Roll The Dice

B Baskerville

Hyem Books

- Chapter 1 -

The yew tree is a complicated plant. To some, a symbol of immortality; to others, an omen of doom. This is a tree that lives so long it must endure nine hundred years to earn the title of *ancient*. There are yew trees in England that took root in Neolithic times, and yet the Romans believed they grew in hell.

Harbingers of death, yew trees are associated with churchyards, the plague, and the longbow. The longbow, England's traditional weapon of choice, was almost exclusively made from yew and was responsible for ending lives from the Bronze Age to the Battle of Flodden.

It made sense that such a tree would grow in the grounds of Fletcher Blackburn's home, for he was a complicated man from a family whose roots, he was certain, began in hell.

This past winter had been cruel to Fletcher's old yew. It stood at the bottom of an expansive garden and cast almost no shadow now that the summer sun was high in the sky. Fletcher Blackburn didn't know how old the yew was, but he knew it had survived two world wars and that his grandma had told him she'd climbed right to the very top when she was a wee whippersnapper. Granny Blackburn had passed on over twenty years ago. Still, the memory of being able to climb trees like a worry-free child must have seemed like another lifetime to the arthritic shell she'd become in her final years. So frail and isolated.

Yes, winter had been cruel to the old tree, but not as cruel as this summer had been to Fletcher. He felt a great compassion for the yew, for he also knew what it felt like to be a shadow of one's former self, to be weak and helpless after a lifetime of standing tall, to be a victim of a force he had not seen coming.

In his early fifties and struggling to breathe, Fletcher didn't feel like himself. He still saw himself as a strapping twenty-something, third in line to the Blackburn empire and feared by all who met him. *He* had been the omen of doom. But as time went on and he ascended the throne, the closer he was watched by the authorities and the fewer people he found he could trust. That was the cruelty of life; the more power you had, the less you could use it.

They say lightning never strikes twice, but it had for the ancient yew, and it had for Fletcher Blackburn. The yew was scorched twice by lightning bolts during a terrible storm one violent night in January. Fletcher, however, had been hit twice by

10mm bullets fired from a Glock .29 less than a minute ago.

Shot with his own gun. In his own study.

Fletcher lay on the floor, his cheek pressed into the white carpet of his home office. His new wife had chosen the carpet. *She'll never get the stain out*, he thought, blinking warily at the yew through a floor-to-ceiling window. The yew, along with the lawn and the flower beds, was tinted yellow. Did the world turn yellow for everyone on their death bed? Had it for Granny? He could feel blood oozing from his chest, his heart slowing, his breathing becoming laboured. His lungs were filling with blood, but he lacked the strength to cough it up. He could feel himself drowning. He didn't have long.

The sound of Mo's standard-issue boots thundering through the hall was a comfort. Mo could handle this; he was armed and medically trained. The door swung open, but there was no sound as Mo checked the room. He moved slowly and silently with his weapon drawn. Reflected in the glass of the windowpane, Fletcher could see his attacker crouched under the desk, concealed from view. He tried to warn Mo. He began to speak but only spluttered blood. Mo crept further into the room, and a shot rang out. Mo fell, his body slamming to the floor like the yew's branch had when it was severed by lightning. No one could help him now.

Fletcher blinked again at the old yew. It was scorched and missing branches and its thick knotted trunk was split in two. But despite its injuries, the tree lived on. Blossom flowers had come and gone, and in a few months, the tree would produce tiny, red berries. The tree had outlived his grandparents and his parents, now it would outlive him. The symbol of immortality would endure. Fletcher Blackburn would not.

- Chapter 2 -

A diamond-white Mercedes convertible surged west on the B6431, a road that connects two of Northumberland's most impressive buildings: Cragside Mansion and Alnwick Castle. To the west, the home of scientist and philanthropist, Lord Armstrong, was the first in the world to be lit using hydroelectric power. Amongst his many esteemed guests were the Shah of Persia and the King of Siam. To the east, Alnwick Castle has, for at least seven hundred years, been the home of the earls and dukes of Northumberland. Though, perhaps it is best known for featuring in the first two Harry Potter films.

Between these two architectural masterpieces, lies another awe-inspiring building. Tucked away in dense woodland, where no one would think to look for it, Morshaw Manor has one foot in the past, one in the future. Constructed in 1901 and retaining many of its original features, Morshaw had been updated with the best in home security, from cameras and sensors to dogs and an armed guard. It was a fortress—or a prison—depending on who you asked.

The convertible slowed as a junction approached. Two women, a blonde and a brunette, finished belting out the latest Mark Ronson hit. The wind tussled loose strands of the brunette's wavy hair, and she fought to push them back behind her ears while the blonde concentrated on the road ahead.

"Thanks again for dinner," the brunette said, turning to face her step-mother who was at the wheel. "And the spa treatments."

"Thank *you* for suggesting it, Lily." Charlene Blackburn turned the car off the main road and onto an unmarked trail that headed towards woodland.

It was still a bright, sunny day, despite the clock reading seven forty-five. Darkness wouldn't arrive until well after ten and the sky would lighten again before four. Long summer days were one of the best things about living in the north, thought Lily. They were up there with the endless beaches and the magnificent castles that dotted the landscape. Lily Blackburn was no fool; she knew everyone thought of her as a materialistic princess. Perhaps part of it was true. But beneath the gel nails, designer bags and influencer status, she was a home bird who loved her little corner of Northumberland.

Charlene patted Lily's knee, "It's been nice to spend some time with you. I feel like we've been so busy; we've hardly had a chance to catch up."

Lily's body stiffened. She had nothing against Charlene, but something inside her twisted whenever she tried to go into step-mother mode. She was not, and would never be, her mother. She was only five years older than her for Christ's sake. Quite what her father saw in her, she'd never know. No, scratch that, she knew *exactly* what her father saw in Charlene. A bubbly demeanour, youthful complexion, and colossal tits. She was the polar opposite of Lily's birth mother, not that Lily considered Hazel to be much of a mother either. Hazel left when Lily was emerging into adulthood. When she'd needed her most. Her parents divorced, Hazel moved to Turkey, and Lily was left at Morshaw Manor with only her dad and older brothers for company.

Charlene may have sensed the change in Lily for she put her hand firmly back on the steering wheel. Pine-shaped shadows engulfed the car as they approached the edge of the wood. Charlene pressed a button on the dashboard, and the car's roof began to move back into place. "How was your head massage?" she asked.

"Heaven," replied Lily, though her tone was flat. "And the salmon blini were to die for."

Charlene let out an orgasmic groan. "Oh, the blinis were absolutely amazing, weren't they?"

"Blini," corrected Lily. "One blin, two blini."

"Huh?" said Charline. "Well, you learn something new every day."

Charlene continued to waffle on about how gifted her masseuse was and about the quality of Kir Royale the hotel had served, but as the car was enveloped by woodland, Lily's thoughts wandered beyond the trees to cloudless Antalya where she wondered if her birth mother would let her come and live with her. Even for just the winter.

Morshaw Manor loomed in the distance, gloomy and ivy-covered. Charlene slowed the car as they approached a set of tall gates. A security system registered the number plate, and the gates automatically opened for the two Blackburn women. Lily's eyes turned to the camera fixed on the gatepost. Usually, it would train on cars as they entered the property, but not today. Today, the camera remained stationary. Charlene parked the E-class cabriolet on the drive and lowered her brow. "Where's Mo?" she asked, staring at the spot where her husband's trusted security guard usually stood.

"Maybe he's on a break?"

Charlene checked her watch. "It's not prayer time." She bit her lip and added, "Did you notice the camera didn't move?"

"Yeah," Lily replied. "Like I said, Mo's probably just on a break?" The brunette gracefully emerged from the car and began to stroll towards the manor, but the blonde remained hesitantly by her vehicle.

"What if something's happened?"

"Like what?"

"Like someone came looking for your dad? An associate or something?"

There was something in the way Charlene said the word *associate* that made Lily pout and shake her head. "Dad runs a taxi firm and a chain of restaurants."

Charlene wavered again then murmured, "Sometimes you can be so naive."

"Look, if you're feeling spooked, I can call Dylan."

"No," Charlene snapped. Her eyes not moving from the front door. "Your brother's resting. He won't want us bothering him."

"You don't have to flinch every time I say Dylan's name, you know? He's not a monster." *Though he might look like one,* she added silently.

Lily huffed and walked back towards Charlene, she linked her arm in that of her step-mother's and walked her to the house. "I think you need something stronger than a Kir Royale. We'll get our PJs on and I'll fix us some brandies." She pressed her thumb onto a fingerprint reader and waited for the click. "We can drink them in the back garden and see if the vixen and her cubs make an appearance."

Lily pushed open the front door to Morshaw Manor, but her hands immediately sprang back to cover her ears. Charlene's scream pierced the air as she forced her way past Lily, skidding towards the door at the end of the hallway and the pool of blood that seeped out from under it.

- Chapter 3 -

Toponymy is the study of place names and their origins. In the United Kingdom, the suffix *ham*, as in Nottingham or Tottenham, refers to a farm. The suffix *wick*, as in Berwick or Keswick, represents a bay. The suffix *shaw*, as in Morshaw Manor, refers to woodland. This isn't a surprise given the thick greenery surrounding the home, but more unsettling is the prefix *mor*, which depicts death. The Blackburns live in Death Woods.

Lily couldn't get to Charlene in time. All the colour drained from the smaller woman's face as she raced along the hallway to the study door. Lily grabbed her hand just as she pulled open the door and the full horror of what lay within was revealed.

"Mo! Oh, dear God. Mo! He's been shot, Lily. He's been shot. Look at him."

Mo's Asian skin tone had faded to ashen and his eyes, though cloudy, were open and staring up at Lily. She shuddered and covered her mouth with her free hand. Blood had pooled from his chest, coating his white shirt with scarlet. There was blood under his head; his scarred fingers still wrapped around the grip of a handgun. The fabric of one trouser leg bunched up over his boot, revealing the lustrous titanium of a prosthetic leg.

The room looked as if someone had taken a pot of red paint and thrown it around like Jackson Pollock. Blood covered the white carpet, seeping into its plush pile and staining it all shades of red from darkest burgundy to palest pink. It dribbled down the walls, speckled the window and painted the air with the sickly smell of copper.

Charlene dived to Mo's side and she touched his cheek. "Mo. Come on, Mo." She pulled her jumper off and began pressing it onto the wound on Mo's chest.

Lily wrapped her arms around Charlene and heaved her back to her feet. "That's not going to help. It's too late." Her voice shook as she added, "We shouldn't touch anything. We should phone the police."

"Police?" Charlene laughed manically. "Police are not welcome in Fletcher Blackburn's home." As she spat the words, they became caught in her throat. "Where is Fletcher? FLETCHER?" she yelled to the ceiling. "FLETCHER?" Then they saw it. The body of the man they both loved lay lifeless and blood-soaked on the floor behind the desk. His head was turned to face the window and the garden he'd cared so much for. "Oh."

Charlene's knees buckled, along with Lily's, and they wailed into each other until a shadow formed over their shoulders. They turned to look, shaking as their eyes crept up the man of six-foot-four until they reached a face carved from a life of violence. His frame was imposing, and his aura suggested a man never to be crossed. His mouth formed a thin line as he looked around the room, then he slowly turned his gaze down to the two fragile women.

DETECTIVE CHIEF INSPECTOR ERICA Cooper was on her first real date in a long time. Lobo Rojo was buzzing. The Mexican restaurant on the fish quay of North Shields was alive with all manner of folk from groups of teens, to octogenarian couples, and every age in between. There was a hum of panting mouths as brave souls poured hot sauce on freshly prepared tacos and deep sighs as chilled margaritas soothed fiery tongues.

"How's the fish?" asked the man sat opposite Cooper. On paper, he should have been perfect for her.

"It's great," Cooper answered, dabbing her mouth with a napkin and taking another look at her date.

Olly Timms, at thirty-six, was close in age to Cooper. He worked as a lawyer in the city-centre and owned a semi-detached in Gosforth. Guardian of domestic abuse victims, Olly specialised in defending women who killed in self-defence and assisted in divorces where one party used or threatened violence against the other. A lot of his work was *pro bono;* the rest of the time he charged a fortune. He was intelligent, a fan of metal music, and he was yet to make a derogatory comment about Cooper's buzzcut.

"Though, given its location," continued Cooper, "if the fish was anything less than stellar it would be criminal."

Olly sipped a beer and nudged his knee against hers under the table. "Well, if you need to sue them... I know a good lawyer." He gave a coy smile then corrected himself. "But you've probably got it covered."

Cooper inched her chair back so their knees wouldn't touch. Olly was good looking. That was beyond doubt. With thick mahogany hair, cut into a professional style, and eyes so dark even the most hardened of people could get lost in them, he was a pretty boy. Cooper liked his looks, his taste in music and the fact he had an autistic younger brother whom he spoke so highly of. He was great, but there was one problem, and it was a major problem: he wasn't Justin Atkinson.

The truth pained her. She wasn't over Atkinson and as long as that was the case, dating was a waste of everyone's time.

Cooper adjusted her weight. "Listen, Olly..."

Her date's face read like a book. *Here we go.*

"Look, I've had a lovely time tonight but—"

"Yeah, *it's not you, it's me,*" he said, making air quotes. "Heard it before. Except it's usually bollocks."

"It's not bollocks," Cooper protested, taking a swig of Corona. "And it is actually me." Before she could continue, her phone rang. She'd have thought, *thank God*, but she'd left it on full volume, causing the entire restaurant to turn and eyeball her. "It's my boss," she whispered apologetically. "Sir?"

Cooper pressed her phone as hard as she could to her ear and jammed a finger in the other one to blot out the sounds of Mexican music, chatter and crockery. Detective Chief Superintendent Howard Nixon sounded worried. Something serious had happened. She got to her feet, mouthed *Sorry*, dropped two twenty-pound notes on the table and hurried from Lobo Rojo.

JUSTIN ATKINSON, ONE OF the most senior scene of crime officers in the region, stood outside Morshaw Manor and checked his watch; it was gone half-ten. Dressed in a white overall and blue plastic booties, he pulled the hood on his fetching outfit down and relished the cooling night breeze on his forehead and cheeks.

"Here." Hong Evanstad, fellow SOCO, handed Atkinson a cup of coffee.

"Thanks." Atkinson thought of the time and asked, "Is this decaf?"

"Absolutely."

"You're such a liar. I'll never sleep if I drink caffeine at this hour."

Hong blew his floppy fringe from his forehead and eyed his superior. "You honestly think you'll get to bed before lunchtime tomorrow?"

He had a point.

"Did you hear the latest?" Hong continued. "Seems we're being Americanised. Can't say I like it."

Atkinson shifted his weight to his other leg. The aches and pains from his pre-dawn run had kicked in and his legs were seizing up. Muscle soreness had never bothered him in his thirties; it had been more of a badge of honour then. If you weren't sore, you hadn't run fast enough. But lately, it wasn't just his muscles that ached; his joints were feeling the strain. When had he become so old? He knew exactly when. It was the moment he'd broken up with Erica Cooper. She'd made him feel young, and without her, he was back to being a greying, forty-something, divorcé who lived to work rather than worked to live. "What do you mean *Americanised*?"

"The higher-ups want a change of name. We're going to be CSIs."

Atkinson winced. "What's wrong with SOCOs?" he asked. He hated change for the sake of change. Next thing you knew, the Queen would be ousted, the Prime Minister would be President, inspectors would be sheriffs and we'd all be ditching tea in favour of— He looked down at his coffee and laughed at himself.

"Got to admit, CSI sounds cooler." Hong put on his best northern English accent, not an easy task when you were Korean by birth and Norwegian by adoption. "Previously on *CSI Newcastle...*"

Atkinson laughed and cast his eyes out over the driveway and surrounding woodland. Other than the glow from the house behind them and the lights from their mobile forensic units, the place was eerily dark. Trees blocked out most of the moonlight, and with the absence of street lighting, the area was imposingly black. "What time did they say this bloodstain expert was going to get here?"

Hong shrugged. "Can't be long now. We requested him as soon as we arrived on site." He checked a small spiral notepad that he kept in his trouser pocket. "Ronnie Rogers. Sounds like he should be in porn, not forensics. Anyway, he's the best Greater Manchester Police could spare."

"Well, we don't see many shootings in our neck of the woods—"

"Neck?" The Korean-Norwegian furrowed his brow.

"It's an expression. Though now I come to think of it, it doesn't make much sense, does it?" He sipped his rapidly cooling coffee. "What I meant was, we don't see many shootings around here, so I'm happy to bring in someone with more expertise in the field."

"Even if they're a stuffy old Oxbridge grad?"

"Even if he wears a tweed jacket with elbow patches."

In the distance, two white headlights pierced the darkness, and the rumble of tyres on gravel could be heard as a classic MG convertible grumbled up the driveway.

"I knew his car would be bottle green," Hong said with an eye roll.

Atkinson and Hong approached the car to welcome their new colleague from the west. The car door opened and they stopped in their tracks. Ronnie Rogers was no tweed-wearing, stuffy, old academic. A perfectly manicured hand extended towards Atkinson and a bright smile lit up the darkness.

"Veronica Rogers," she said through lips the colour of merlot. "But please, call me Ronnie."

"SHE SMELLS LIKE ROSEMARY and lavender and all things good in the world," said Hong in a whisper from behind his forensics mask.

"Behave," warned Atkinson, though he thoroughly agreed. Ronnie Rogers smelled like Eden.

"That raven hair. That milky skin..."

"Don't come crying to me if you're sacked for sexual misconduct."

Ronnie looked up from behind her camera. "Who's been sacked for sexual misconduct?" she asked.

"No one," they answered in unison.

Atkinson shoved Hong in the ribs as a warning to keep his hormones in check and approached Ronnie as she continued to work. She'd photographed the scene from every angle imaginable and was about to start placing little markers wherever she thought more examination was necessary.

"Who has the bodies?" she asked.

"They're at the morgue. Freeman Hospital in Newcastle. Margot Swanson will take care of them."

"She any good?"

"She's excellent," Atkinson confirmed.

"I'd like to see the photographs of the victims from when they were still in situ."

"Of course," he replied. "I have them on my laptop. We took 3D images as well."

Ronnie nodded. "Good. The victims were shot from different directions and different heights. I can tell by the forward spatter. That's the blood as it leaves the exit wounds, but you don't need me to tell you that."

She stood on her tiptoes and aimed an imaginary gun towards a section of blood-soaked carpet by the window. Then she turned and crouched, looking back towards the door where pink misting covered a part of the wall and a swipe mark ran to the floor. "Any sign of the gun?"

"No. We've done a basic sweep but will continue in the morning. We found 10mm casings. Winchester Silvertips."

She nodded again. "That makes sense," she mused, taking a closer look at how some blood trailed down a standing lamp. "The victim by the window was shot in the chest. The victim by the door was shot in the torso then the head."

With the absence of bodies, Atkinson wondered how she could know so much already. "Did Hong tell you that?"

"No," Ronnie said with a glint in her eye. "The blood did, and blood never lies."

- Chapter 4 -

Almost three and a half thousand police officers make up Northumbria Police, making it the sixth-largest force in England and Wales. Several of those three and half thousand had been awoken earlier than planned. They washed, dressed and assembled in the force's headquarters on Middle Engine Lane in an area called Wallsend.

Four a.m. and despite the yawns, heads resting on desks, and sleep being picked from eyes, the incident room was filled with a quiet buzz. This was a big one; they could all feel it. There was electricity in the air. Journalists were going to wake to one of the biggest stories of the year, and careers were going to be made—or broken—on how everyone involved played it.

DCI Erica Cooper looked vastly different to how she had just hours earlier. Gone was the Keith Flint t-shirt and leather trousers she'd worn on her date. She'd opted for a tailored grey suit and the highest heels she could wear without wanting to amputate her feet after four hours. Cooper wasn't a stranger to wearing casual clothes to work. She often opted for jeans and flats, so were the perks of being plain-clothed, but on certain days you had to look the part, and today was one of those days. She opened a manilla folder as the sounds of the room dimmed to hushed whispers and pinned two photographs to the murder wall.

"Thank you for coming in so early," she said, addressing the room as one. "Last night, Fletcher Blackburn, fifty-two, acting head of the Blackburn family, was executed in his own home: Morshaw Manor."

Almost everyone in the room adjusted their weight, or sat up straighter, or scratched an itch they didn't know was there until now. "SOCO worked through the night in Fletcher's home office—that's the kill site—and will continue with the rest of the house and the grounds today. They've also brought in a bloodstain analyst from Greater Manchester Police. The murder weapon, a handgun, has yet to be found. Now, none of you will need our oleaginous friend in local intelligence..." Cooper cringed at the thought of local intelligence officer, Cedric Bell, and saw that DS Paula Keaton was sporting a grossed-out expression of her own, "...to tell you that Fletcher's brother, Eddie Blackburn, was head of the Blackburns until a certain someone," she motioned to herself, "made him sing like a canary and found him a new home at HMP Frankland."

There was a wave of smiles across the room as they all flashed back with nostalgia. A lone hand shot up from the back of the room.

"Yes, Boyd?" Cooper asked, acknowledging the newest face in the department.

DC Saffron Boyd blushed as the eyes of the room turned to her. "I'm afraid I'm not familiar with the Blackburns, ma'am."

"Ah, yes. Lucky you." Cooper extended an arm towards the new DC. "Everyone, this is DC Boyd. DC Boyd, this is everyone. Boyd recently transferred from West Yorkshire. I'll get a file put together to bring you up to speed. In the meantime, let me sum it up as follows..." Cooper perched on the edge of her desk and took a deep breath. "The Blackburns are a crime family known for drug distribution, prostitution, dogfighting, gambling syndicates, and extortion. Did I miss anything, Paula?"

DS Paula Keaton stifled a yawn. "Bare-knuckle boxing and counterfeit handbags, boss."

Cooper nodded at the woman who was twice the size she was. "Now Eddie liked to keep his hands clean, laundering money through a chain of pizzerias and a taxi firm. The NCA were after him for years, then one day, a pub up in Amble called the Harbour Lights went up in flames, and it burnt to the ground with two people inside it. Well, it fell into my lap, but the NCA were tripping over their dicks trying to take the case off me. Eddie's son was implicated, but I kept Theo out of it on the condition that Eddie told us everything he knew about the Daytons. The Daytons, for those of you who aren't familiar, are another criminal family and plague to the north-east. Eddie went to jail, and the NCA got a boatload of intel. Win, win. With Eddie safe and sound in Frankland, baby brother Fletcher rose to head of the family." Cooper pointed to his photograph. "Right, get your pens ready."

Everyone in the room opened their notepads and sat poised like good little schoolboys and girls.

"Fletcher Blackburn's manor home is situated in the woodland northeast of Cragside. Two hectares of land surrounded by eight-foot walls and security cameras. There's one road in unless you want a mile trek through the undergrowth and can climb like Spiderman. He's on his second marriage. Married to twenty-six-year-old Charlene Blackburn."

Cooper pinned a photo of a Barbie-like blonde next to the one of Fletcher. Murmurs about trophy wives and gold diggers floated through CID until Cooper coughed loudly. "He has three children from his first marriage: Dylan, George and Lily. I've never had the pleasure, but from what I hear, Dylan is the brawn, George is the brains and Lily is the beauty."

DS Jack Daniel folded his long legs and held his pen above his head of dark blond curls. "Who found the bodies?"

"That would be Lily and Charlene. They came home just before eight. Dylan appeared when he heard the screaming."

"You mean he was at home?" asked the detective known as Tennessee due to his distinctive name.

"Indeed he was."

Tennessee shrugged. "This seems pretty open and closed."

"Looks that way," Cooper confirmed, "but there are plenty of people who'd like to harm the Blackburns. Rivals, former employees, vengeful relatives of cannon fodder. We'll need to do some brainstorming."

"So who's that guy?" Tennessee pointed with his pen at the photograph of the second victim.

Cooper turned to Keaton. "Want to take this?"

Keaton cleared her throat, though there was no need; when Keaton spoke, people listened. "Ibrahim Moradi. Known as Mo. Born and raised in Bradford. Parents own a restaurant, brother owns a carpet shop. Ibrahim's ex-army. He served two tours in Afghanistan before being medically discharged after losing his foot to a landmine. Competed in the Invictus Games in 2018, winning bronze in the shot-put. Even got to shake Prince Harry's hand."

No one looked impressed. His achievements were tarnished by any association to the Northumbrian mafia.

"From what I've been told by the first responders, Lily and Charlene confirmed that Ibrahim worked as Fletcher's security guard. He monitored the front gates by CCTV and basically made sure no one came to the house without permission. Fletcher's inner circle was very small by all accounts. Few people were allowed in the house unless it was by prior arrangement."

"Any sign of forced entry?" Tennessee asked.

"None."

"So someone with access, presumably Dylan, overpowered Ibrahim to get to Fletcher?".

"That seems the most likely," Cooper answered.

"Okay. So what's the plan?"

Cooper closed her file and surveyed the room. "Tennessee, you're with me."

The younger DS smiled. He was usually at Cooper's side and didn't like it any other way.

"We'll head to Morshaw, speak with forensics and have a walkthrough of the scene. I want to know everything. Keaton and Martin, I need you two to head to Budle Bay. The family are staying in a property they own. Have a chat but handle them with kid gloves. These people hate the police. We're the enemy and they won't trust us. Keep it friendly and chatty. Get alibis in the most informal, relaxed way you can. If we push too hard, they'll shut us out, decide on their own who's guilty and hand out their own form of punishment."

Keaton saluted and turned to the young DC on her left. Oliver Martin liked to take care of his appearance. Even at this ungodly hour he'd styled his hair and dressed in the best suit he could afford. He looked back at Keaton and gave her a fist bump.

"Boyd, meet Elliot Whyte."

Nixon had given Cooper some extra manpower. She'd have preferred to have picked her own team, but beggars couldn't be choosers. Boyd and Whyte were free, so Boyd and Whyte were who she'd ended up with.

Saffron Boyd twitched a nervous smile at a large man in his thirties. He had heavy, dark brows and an aquiline nose. Boyd, conversely, was rather mousy in her appearance with light brown hair and wide eyes. Whyte looked like he could swoop down and carry her off to his nest at any moment. There had been many a rumour about Boyd since her transfer from West Yorkshire less than a week ago. Cooper didn't know if any or all of them were true, nor did she care. If Boyd had been sleeping with the superintendent, it was none of her business. As someone who had suffered more than her fair share of rumours spread about her, Cooper had no interest in discussing the matter. Whyte, on the other hand, she had known from way back in the day. Cooper and he had been on the same intake. That didn't mean she liked him.

"Elliot's new to CID but he's been with Northumbria Police since he was twenty-one. He knows the lay of the land. I want you two to speak to the neighbours, granted they're at least a mile away, but see if anything unusual happened last night."

"Yes, ma'am," Boyd replied, her face stony and all business.

Keaton leant back in her chair, balancing it on its two back legs, and in a stage whisper said, "The boss hates the M-word. Stick with Coop or boss if you don't want to end up doing all the grunt work."

Boyd's creamy complexion flushed red. "Sorry, boss."

"Paula," Cooper warned. "Stop scaring the new kids. As for the rest of you, what are you waiting for? You know what to do."

THE WESTGATE UNIT WITHIN HMP Frankland was a prison within a prison. Deep behind the walls and razor wire, beyond the patrolling guards and hefty German shepherds, lay a unit for the demons of society. Westgate was one of only four DSPD units in the country and catered for the nation's prisoners who displayed Dangerous Severe Personality Disorders.

Prison Officer Gareth Finch tapped on a heavy door and peered through the bars of its small window.

"What?" came the sullen reply.

"Sorry to wake you, Eddie," Gareth said in hushed tones. Why did he have to draw the short straw? *Shit.* Talk about shooting the messenger. "You have a phone call. You should take it."

Eddie Blackburn rolled to his side and threw his blanket to the floor. He stood, displaying his naked body to Gareth without any hint of shame. "What time is it?" he asked.

"Almost five."

"Fuck me." Eddie ran a hand over his face and pulled on a pair of orange trousers. Meanwhile, Gareth fumbled with the lock to his cell and tightly held his baton. At the slightest hint of trouble, the cavalry would come running, not that it made him feel any better. He'd served in Westgate for three years now and knew how much damage could be caused in only a few seconds given the right prisoner.

EDDIE WALKED AHEAD AND lifted a handset from one of the telephones mounted to a wall in the communal area. He hated this fucking place with every fibre of his being. He hated the cells, the so-called gym, the other inmates and the bloody screws. At least the screws had the good sense to treat him with an ounce of respect. Some of the inmates were a few too many fries short of a Happy Meal to know what was good for them. He didn't belong here with the murderers, rapists and terrorists. Eddie wasn't any of those things. Okay, he'd killed before, but in his defence, he'd been provoked. He wasn't one of these fruit cakes who shat up the walls just for the stinkin' hell of it.

"Hello?" he said as the line connected.

Eddie listened to every word as a panicked voice squealed down the phone. He noted the screw moving a few steps away from him. Eddie remembered his little brother as an innocent five-year-old when they'd snuck out to the department store to sit on Santa's knee and ask for Pa to stop hitting Ma. He thought of his little brother on his wedding day, blissfully happy at the thought of being shacked up with that miserable bitch, Hazel. Then he thought of Mo. He knew Mo and trusted him. No one got into Morshaw Manor without Fletcher's say so, not even Eddie. This was a betrayal.

Eddie replaced the handset and walked back to his cell without saying a word. As the door locked behind him, he slid his hand into his trouser pocket and felt the sharp edge of the shank. Betrayals were only handled one way in the Blackburn family.

- Chapter 5 -

The sun had been up for an hour by the time Cooper and Tennessee arrived at Morshaw, and it still wasn't close to breakfast time. Cooper parked a few meters from the police tape and stared ahead at a forensics unit. The shiny BMW she now drove had once belonged to a former colleague. DI Sam Sutherland had been sentenced to eleven years for kidnapping and people trafficking, and the only good thing to come out of the whole sorry affair was Cooper's ability to buy his car at auction for a fraction of its worth. She missed her old colleague. He'd been a father figure, a shoulder to cry on, and a good detective. But she couldn't forgive him, nor would she ever visit him in the category C prison to which he'd been sent. Her actual father meanwhile, was living the high life in Lanzarote. Cooper hoped to visit him and her mother at Christmastime. By the time December got here, she'd be in dire need of some vitamin D and one of her father's famous sangrias.

"Things still awkward?" Tennessee asked.

Cooper blinked then followed his gaze. He was nodding his head towards where tall, silver-haired Justin Atkinson was balancing two hot drinks on a tray.

"Oh," she said, pushing fathers, real and surrogate from her mind. "Very."

"You know, if you want, I can—"

"Don't even think about it," Cooper said, cutting across him. Her heart was suddenly racing. "If you think for a second I'm going to ask you to take over the running of this walkthrough so that I don't have to make uncomfortable small talk with my ex you are wildly mistaken."

"Sorry, Coop." Tennessee looked terrified of the tiny ball of fury sat next to him. "I didn't mean you weren't capable of doing your job or owt, I just thought I'd save you the weirdness."

"Weirdness? I'm DCI. My work is twenty-four-seven weirdness. If I palmed off every task I didn't want to do, I'd never do anything."

"Sorry, Coop," Tennessee repeated.

"Ah. Forget it. I'm not angry at you. I'm angry at..." Her voice trailed away as she buried her frustrations. Why did Sutherland have to go and do what he did? If he'd just come to her for help, he'd still be on the team, and Elliot Whyte would still be under whatever rock he'd crawled out from. Cooper swallowed and checked her reflection in the car's vanity mirror. She looked good. Well, she looked average, but that was good for someone who'd been up all night and was fostering a great deal of resentment. At least she didn't have to see Justin Atkinson while looking like a complete emotional mess. She snapped the visor back into place and exited the car with a false pep in her step. She rounded the forensics van to find Atkinson giggling away with a woman who had the striking dark features and grace of a Jordanian princess. Cooper might look good all things considered, but she didn't look Jordanian-princess-good.

Atkinson and the beauty looked up from their pop-up stools, and Atkinson jumped to his feet, spilling tea all over his giggle-buddy.

"Erica," he greeted, ambling towards her.

"Justin. We must stop meeting like this." A shoddy attempt at light-hearted humour.

Atkinson laughed through his nose and shook hands with the two detectives.

"So, who's the new girl?" Cooper asked, casting a look beyond Atkinson's left shoulder.

"Girl? Well, woman, surely. She's thirty-six."

The woman was older than Cooper but had no lines or bags under her eyes. *Bitch.* Botox. It had to be botox.

"She's Veronica Rogers," Justin continued. "Head of bloodstain analysis for Greater Manchester. We needed more grey matter on this one."

Of course, she was also a genius. Cooper listened to her spiteful inner monologue and told herself to shut the hell up. She'd just told Tennessee she was capable of doing her job like a grown-up and yet, on the inside, she was acting like a catty sixteen-year-old.

"Shall we?" she asked, nodding towards the house. It pained Cooper that illegal activities and exploitation could buy such a breathtaking home. Up and down the country people were working long, hard days in honest jobs for minimum wage. Many of them struggled to get a foot the housing ladder.

Atkinson handed her and Tennessee protective clothing and shoe covers and led the way through a swarm of men and women in similar outfits. When he reached the door to Fletcher's home office, he pushed it open and waited for their reactions.

"Christ," was all Tennessee could mutter. His eyes flicked around the room, darting from one drop of blood to the next, and his lip curled at the sight of something congealed on a lampshade.

"That's brain tissue from the second victim," Atkinson explained. "If you were wondering."

The colour drained from the DS's face, so much so he looked almost green. "I wasn't, but thank you."

Cooper wasn't as squeamish as Tennessee, but she was still taken aback by what she saw. In her years in CID, she'd seen many a murder scene but very few shootings, and even fewer where brain matter had blown out the back of a victim's head.

"Fletcher was here," Atkinson said, pointing to a taped off area of carpet next to the window. "And Ibrahim was over here."

Cooper looked past the tape, into the garden. A tree that had seen better days looked like it had been set fire to at some point. A flower bed with snapdragons, delphiniums, peonies and foxgloves caught her eye; a colourful and cheerful distraction from the horror indoors. She looked around the room again and frowned at the mayhem that was the home office. Files were strewn about the place, a tub of pens had been upended and a chair lay on its side. A vase was shattered on the floor and though the water it contained had since dried into the carpet, the peonies it had held, presumably from the garden, were left to wilt on the floor. She stuck her head back into the hallway and scanned about. In contrast to the office, everything was as you would expect. Nothing seemed out of place. She wandered further down the hall and peered into a lounge area and an impressive kitchen. Nothing broken. No sign of a struggle.

She returned to Tennessee's side. "We were wrong about Ibrahim being overpowered to get to Fletcher. There's no suggestion of anything untoward anywhere but in here."

"That fits with what Atkinson just told me," he replied, looking to the SOCO to repeat himself.

"Ah, yes, as I was saying. Ronnie, that's Veronica, found blood spatter from Ibrahim that extended over the trousers of Fletcher." He pointed to a trail of blood droplets that cut through the carpet from near the lamp to the window. "If Ibrahim had been killed first, his blood would be under Fletcher's body, not over it. Fletcher was killed first."

"So, our killer either snuck past the security detail, or they had permission to be here?"

"Like the son who was supposedly asleep upstairs?" Tennessee asked.

Atkinson took a closer look at a book that had fallen off the bookcase. "I can't help you with that. But I can tell you Fletcher was shot from a height, roughly about here." He stood on his tiptoes and aimed his fingers as if they were a gun towards the desk. "Fletcher was shot once here, just above the desk. He was either sitting on it or standing in front of it. Then he either fell over it or was pushed off it, and as he was lying on the carpet over here, he was shot again."

Cooper scribbled down notes as he spoke.

"Ronnie will string the room up once we've finished collecting our samples and she'll be able to give you a much more accurate idea of height. Almost the opposite happened with Ibrahim. He was shot from low to high."

"The killer was hiding under the desk?" Cooper asked.

"Perhaps. It's a pretty big desk. I'd fit under it quite comfortably."

Tennessee bobbed his head as he often did when trying to visualise something. "Okay. So our killer is in here with Fletcher. There's a scuffle. He shoots him on or near the desk, then again when he's on the floor. The guard hears the commotion and the gunfire and comes running. The killer hides under the desk or is crouched next to Fletcher, and he shoots Ibrahim as he enters the room. Any prints?"

Atkinson chuckled. "Loads. I've taken prints from the wife, daughter and two sons. We'll start by eliminating them and see what's left."

"Footprints?" Cooper asked, her eyes turning down to the floor.

"Yes and no."

"What do you mean?"

"Someone stepped in Fletcher's blood. Presumably, it was the killer as Ibrahim didn't get that far into the room. They scrubbed it though, so it's just a blurry, bloody mess. We can't gauge shoe size or even type from it."

"What did they scrub it with?" Cooper asked.

"I don't know. We haven't found any bloody rags yet. If I had to guess, I'd say he stepped in the blood as he was climbing out from under the desk, then removed his shoes and tiptoed out of here."

Cooper pouted. "What about toe prints? Are they unique like fingerprints are?"

"Yes, they are indeed. But, the killer was most likely wearing socks, and even if he weren't, I can't lift a toe print from carpet. Hardwood, yes, but most of the house is carpeted."

Cooper huffed through her pouted lips. She'd hoped for something more concrete. "Right, Tennessee, get on to the first responders. They seized the tapes from the CCTV. I was told the tapes were wiped, but get them over to tech and see if they can work a miracle for us. Justin, I assume you've dusted the monitors?" He looked insulted. "Of course you have. Okay, let me know what turns up."

A blast of noise erupted from above them, and all three heads turned to the ceiling.

Hong's voice rang out. "I found a gun!"

- Chapter 6 -

Cooper waited on the upstairs landing. She had to give the scene of crime officers space to work and didn't want to accidentally contaminate any evidence. Still, from the hallway, she had a decent view into a sumptuous bedroom. A wardrobe was open, and numerous suits hung from padded hangers. A framed photograph of Fletcher and Charlene on their wedding day was set on a bedside table along with a copy of a romance novel, a book on landscaping, a Stephen King, an empty wine glass and some expensive-looking hand cream. It was clearly the master bedroom.

A short scene of crime officer with thick glasses pushed past on her way into the room. Cooper pressed her back into the wall to make space. The SOCO was holding a pad of tiny orange stickers and immediately got to work popping them on all surfaces that harboured potential evidence, including the rim of the wine glass.

Another SOCO held a heavy Canon camera and was taking photographs of a dresser. He moved closer so he could angle the camera into one of its drawers. A box was removed which was photographed, opened up and photographed again. Hong removed the gun from the box, slipped it into an evidence bag and carefully labelled it. When he was finished, he turned to another colleague and asked him to get it to the lab as fast as possible for print and DNA analysis.

"Put a rush on it," he added.

Cooper waved at Hong; he saw and motioned for her to enter the room.

"Where did you find it?" she asked.

"In a jewellery box, hidden at the back of Mrs Blackburn's underwear drawer," he held up a microscopic g-string that still had its price tag attached. He peered at it as if examining an alien species. "How come the smallest things cost the most?"

"Beats me." Cooper pulled her phone from her pocket but struggling to operate the touch screen through her gloves, she opted to leave the scene. Finding a gun in Charlene Blackburn's jewellery box was a massive red flag and one she had to deal with straight away. Once outside in the fresh, pine-scented air, she put a call into DS Paula Keaton.

"Boss?"

"What you up to, Paula?"

Keaton's voice was hushed. "We're over at Budle Bay. Been having a chat with the wife. She won't stop crying."

"Charlene? Where is she?"

"She's just nipped to the loo. I told her I'd make a cup of tea while she washes her face. Then I'll try to get her to open up some more."

"Is Martin with you?"

"He's right here."

"Forensics found a gun in Charlene's jewellery box."

Cooper heard what sounded like a teaspoon being dropped on a counter. "Shit. Right, We'll bring her in. See you back at HQ?"

Cooper confirmed then read the messages that had come through on her phone since the morning briefing. Olly Timms, her date from last night, had seen the news and asked if that's why she'd run off in such a hurry. She didn't want to ghost Olly, he was a nice guy, but at the same time, she hardly knew him and didn't owe him a detailed response. She sent a brief reply: *Sorry, can't discuss the case.* He'd understand; he was a lawyer.

She looked up from her phone and turned her attention to Atkinson. He had a laptop set up on a foldable table and was squinting at the screen. Cooper felt a bubble of sadness form in her gut. She should have listened to him when they'd been together. He'd tried to warn her about Tina's father, but she'd been too proud and too stubborn to hear. It was her own damn fault she felt this way.

She forced a smile and approached him. "I'm off now. Thanks for your help." She hoped her voice wasn't too obviously cheery.

He shut the laptop. "Just doing my job."

Cooper swallowed. "It's going to be a long day. Think I'll need a beer when it's finally home time."

"You're telling me."

Did she dare? She did. "Do you have plans?"

Atkinson's mouth opened, then his eyes flicked to where Ronnie Rogers was zipping herself into a forensics suit.

Cooper felt her cheeks burn. How stupid of her.

"Actually... Ronnie asked me to a talk at the City Library. There's a former New York CSI turned best-selling author giving a speech on the true cases that inspired his fiction."

Idiot. "Sounds great," Cooper said with a stammer. She felt like a prize fool and couldn't get out of there fast enough. Luckily, she now had a speedy BMW at her disposal. "Enjoy."

"HOW MANY TIMES DO I have to say it? I've never seen that gun before in my life."

Charlene Blackburn's voice was high-pitched and childlike. It reminded Cooper of Lisa Simpson's voice, had the Simpson's been set in the UK. Charlene didn't look anything like the glamorous image that Cooper had pinned on the murder wall earlier that day. Save for some mascara stains running down her cheeks, Charlene was make-up free. Her thick blonde hair was pulled back in a pony-tail, and wispy baby hairs poked out at all angles from her hairline. She was dressed in a velour tracksuit that, although hideous, probably cost a fortune. Her skin was blotchy from crying and she'd picked away at her gel nails and the surrounding flesh until her fingers were red raw.

Cooper maintained silent eye contact and waited for her interviewee to speak again.

Charlene sniffed and looked back at a photograph that lay on the table in the interview suit. "I told you. I don't recognise that gun. It's not Mo's. Mo uses a... Oh, what did he say it was? A Sig something?"

"A Sig Sauer P320."

"Yes. It's not his. He was— He was still holding the Sig when Lily and I found them." She dabbed the corners of her eyes with her fingertips then squeezed her eyes shut. "I can't get the image out of my head."

Cooper tapped the photograph, causing Charlene to open her eyes again and follow the sound. "This is a Glock .29. The bullet casings match the ones found at the scene. This was the gun used to kill Ibrahim Moradi and your husband, Fletcher Blackburn—"

"And I don't know whose it is—"

"Then why was it hidden in your underwear draw?"

"I don't know! Okay? I don't bloody know!" Her voice was shrill and quivering. "Whoever shot Fletcher must've put it there. They must want to make me look guilty. But I swear to God—" She slammed her hand on the table. "You won't find my prints on that gun."

Charlene was getting irritated; angry people made mistakes.

"Because you wiped it clean?"

"NO!" She slammed her hand down again.

Cooper looked to her left and stroked her cheek with two fingers. It was a coded message to anyone in the observation room that she wanted a coffee. One finger for tea, two fingers for coffee, and three fingers for *someone switch places with me before I lose my shit*.

"Okay, I'll humour you, Charlene." Another comment meant to wind her interviewee up. "Let's make-believe and say you've never seen this gun before and that you've no knowledge of how it could possibly end up in your underwear drawer."

"I haven't."

"Let me finish." Cooper was in no mood for interruptions. "Who would? And why would they want to frame you?"

Charlene looked down at her hands and pulled at a loose bit of cuticle until it snapped and began to bleed. She put her finger in her mouth and sucked it as she spoke. "I... I guess I'm the easiest one to pin it on. I know what they say about me."

"What do they say?"

"That I'm a gold digger."

"Who says that?"

"Well, everyone. But D-Dylan mostly."

"Fletcher's eldest?"

"Yes. That man hates me. He hates everyone. Has a right nasty temper as well."

The door opened, and Oliver Martin entered with coffee in a plastic cup. He placed it on the table and left before Cooper could request a biscuit.

"Why does Dylan hate you?"

Charlene shrugged and cowered into her chair. She examined her finger and balled it inside a fist.

"Do you need a plaster?"

"No, thank you."

"Then I'll ask again. Why does Dylan hate you?"

"I can't blame him. I'm younger than he is. Imagine having a step-mother who's younger than you are. It's got to be weird for him. And after Hazel left, that's Fletcher's ex, he probably thought as eldest he'd... you know... inherit Fletcher's money."

"How do you get on with Fletcher's other children?"

"George and Lily? They're all right. We get on. Well, we do most of the time. They don't call me any names, not to my face anyway. George doesn't say much to me. Half the time, if I walk into a room, he'll walk out. And as for Lily, I don't know, sometimes we're close, like sisters or friends, other times I can tell she wishes Hazel never left, but I... I think George and Lily understand."

"Understand what?" Cooper asked.

"That I love Fletcher. That I'm not with their father for his money. I don't want his stinking money. I just... I just want him back." She opened her hand. Her palm was smeared with blood, and the sight of it caused fresh tears.

Cooper gave her a moment to compose herself again before pressing on. "Charlene, I want to go over everything else that happened that day. You said you'd been for some spa treatments?"

"Yes. At Doxford Hall. Lily and I went for massages. I got my nails done as well." She stopped and looked at the sorry state her manicure was in now. "Then we had dinner and got home at around half eight."

Cooper knew Doxford Hall. She and Atkinson had spent New Years there. They'd walked through snowy woodland until they couldn't feel their toes then returned to sip a delicious red while sharing a warm bath. She couldn't think about that right now.

"And what did you do earlier in the day?"

She looked puzzled. "Erm... It's a bit of a blur really. I slept in, woke up after nine. Paulo was waiting for me."

"Paulo?"

"My pilates instructor. He was waiting in the back garden."

"Full name?" Cooper asked.

"Oh. I'm not sure. I just know him as Pilates Paulo. That's what he goes by on Facebook."

Cooper would check. "Go on."

"We trained for an hour. Paulo left. Then I made a smoothie and had a shower."

"Was anyone else around?"

"George was at home. He was in the kitchen and wanted the blender after I'd finished with it. Fletcher was busy in his office. Mo was watching the cameras. I'm not sure about Lily and Dylan."

Cooper made a note. "And after you showered?"

"I spent a few hours on housework then went shopping."

"Morshaw's a big house. You don't have a cleaner?"

She shook her head. "I don't mind playing house. I find cleaning rather therapeutic."

Cooper stared but said nothing.

"Fletcher doesn't like unnecessary people at Morshaw. He just about tolerates Paulo. He'd never approve of a cleaner."

Cooper cast her mind back to the murder scene. Other than the office, the rest of the house was spotlessly clean. She wondered if the lab would find the gun to be just as clean. "Where did you go shopping?"

"Jesmond. I parked on Acorn Road and went to Peak Boutique then walked to Clayton Road for Designer."

"After that?"

"After that, I drove into town and spent some time in Fenwick, got a latte at Starbucks, then Lily called and we arranged to go for some treatments."

Cooper would have Martin check in with the two Jesmond boutiques as well as the large department store in the city centre. She'd also have him run her plates against the city centre ANPR cameras.

There was a knock on the door to the interview suite. Keaton popped her head around the door. "Got a moment, boss?"

Cooper shuffled her papers back into their file and tucked it under her arm. She picked up her coffee and followed Keaton into the hallway. "What you got?" she asked, knowing Keaton wouldn't interrupt an interview without good reason.

"Two things." She leant against the wall and folded her thick arms over her chest. "Atkinson called, they found a copy of Fletcher's will as well as an entry in his diary that might be of interest."

"Will first," Cooper said, bringing the plastic cup to her lips and taking a sip. The coffee was still scorching. She'd told Martin a thousand times that he should add a touch of cold water to it. The boy needed more training.

"Charlene gets the lot."

"The lot? Nothing goes to the kids?"

"Not a penny," Keaton confirmed, one eyebrow raised high.

"The house is worth over two and a half million, and he's got a life insurance policy valued at six hundred grand."

Cooper whistled. "Nice."

"The restaurants and taxi firm go to Theo, his nephew."

"Yeah. That's Eddie's son."

"Dylan, George and Lily were only entitled to the money if he and Charlene divorced."

Cooper gently blew on her coffee. She'd been up all night and needed the caffeine to be able to function. "Hmm. If the kids knew about the will and were pissed that they wouldn't inherit anything..."

"Then they'd kill Charlene," Keaton suggested.

"Exactly. Why kill their father and frame their step-mother, leaving his estate tied up in legal knots for an age? It doesn't make sense."

Keaton pulled a face. "The things people do never make sense. You know that."

She was right. "So, what was in the diary?"

Keaton unlocked an iPad she was carrying and showed Cooper a photograph that had been emailed to her. Cooper studied the pages of Fletcher Blackburn's diary. It showed a weekly journal spread over two pages.

"*Sunday sixteenth. Drop off dry cleaning. Speak to George regarding Jamison account. Gym at five. Wayne Hanson at six. Call the witch regarding George's birthday*. Who's the witch?"

"I'm guessing the ex-wife," Keaton said with a chuckle. "I'll call Lily or George Blackburn and see if they can confirm."

Cooper continued scanning. "*Monday seventeenth. Family meeting at nine-thirty. Tennis at eleven. Wayne Hanson at two.*" Cooper tried her coffee again; it was just about drinkable. Downing the whole cup and feeling the caffeine hit her system, she widened her eyes and stood up a little taller. "Charlene hasn't mentioned a family meeting on the day her husband was killed."

"He could mean *family,*" Keaton said, making air quotes as she said the word family.

"As in the mafia? As in only those who need to know?"

She shrugged. "It's one explanation."

"And who's Wayne Hanson?" Cooper's brain was firing on all cylinders again; she was sure she knew the name from somewhere. "He met with Fletcher the day before and the day of his murder."

"I'll run the name," Keaton said.

"Good. Something tells me his name will come up in our database."

Keaton locked the iPad's screen and headed for the incident room. Cooper crushed the plastic cup and tossed it in a recycling bin before re-entering the interview suite. She found Charlene Blackburn sobbing into a dirty tissue, her eyes even redder than they had been just minutes before.

"Mrs Blackburn, if you're found not guilty, and that's a big *if* given the murder weapon was in your underwear drawer, you're going to be a seriously wealthy woman." She sat opposite Charlene and waited for her to look up. "Tell me what you know about Fletcher's will."

- Chapter 7 -

THE TIDE WAS IN at Budle Bay, and expansive mudflats were coated in a shallow film of water that shimmered under the summer sun. Sandpipers waded in the brackish water of the estuary where the Waren Burn met the North Sea. An oystercatcher dipped its bright orange beak below the surface and emerged with a mussel.

"I love it up here," Tennessee said as he looked out of the car window. They were driving north, approaching Budle Bay from Bamburgh. Bamburgh was a small village that despite its modest size, was blessed with a gargantuan castle and a beach that seemed to go on forever. It was something that had to be seen to be believed. "Hayley and I used to come hiking here a lot before Alfie was born."

"I heard there's an old World War II bunker around here somewhere?" Cooper glanced left and right as she drove.

"Yeah, it's just up that way on the right," Tennessee answered, pointing towards the sands. "Would have housed a large field gun back in the day to take out any approaching enemy forces." He blushed, then added, "I had sex in there once."

"No!?"

"Yes."

Cooper laughed. "You dirty little bugger."

"Don't tell Alfie, but he might have been conceived there. Was that or the lime kilns on Holy Island."

"And I had you pinned as the gentleman of CID." Cooper shook her head. Then, because she wanted to change the subject, asked, "How is Haley?"

"Some days are better than others. I told you the mother-in-law lives with us now?"

"You did. How's that working out?" Cooper rounded a bend and pulled the car into the driveway of a large barn conversion. Earlier in the year, Hayley Daniel has suffered a crippling case of postnatal depression. Tennessee had been worried she could hurt herself and had taken time off to look after his new family.

"In theory, it's great. Pat gives Hayley the support she needs while I'm working. Plus, Alfie loves her, and it gives Pat something to focus her energy on since her husband passed."

"And in practice?"

Tennessee gave her a look.

Cooper chuckled. "In practice, you're living with your mother-in-law. Say no more."

Cooper's phone began ringing; she selected speakerphone before answering. "Paula?"

"Boss. I've got the info on Wayne Hanson."

"Go on."

"Well, you were right about knowing his name. He's basically Gateshead's version of Blackburn, controlling everything in the triangle between Blaydon, Washington and Jarrow. Nowhere near as prolific as the Blackburns but still dangerous."

"Ah. I know the ones you mean," Tennessee chimed in. "They're big on cockfighting."

"And human cockfighting. Someone died at one of their underground boxing matches last year. The venue owner went down for it in the end. They couldn't prove Hanson had anything to do with it and no one would name the other fighter. Remember Athena Fox? Little blonde fighter from Shields? Helped solve the Tyneside Prowler case?"

"Yeah, I remember," said Cooper. It had been one mighty embarrassment for the force. Numerous young women were assaulted, the police were clueless, and in the end, they had a woman who smiled like an angel but fought like a demon to thank.

"Myers and I investigated a break-in at her home back when I was a DC. Rumour has it, the other fighter was one of the heavyweights from her old gym. Nothing to back it up though. When those guys close ranks, it's like getting blood out of a stone."

"Thanks for doing the research," Cooper said. "You and Martin going to pay Hanson a visit?"

"Already en route."

"Okay. Be careful, Paula."

Cooper heard a grunt before Keaton hung off.

Tennessee exited the passenger side door and took in the barn conversion. It was high-spec, modern, and it obviously cost a pretty penny. "Charlene gets this property as well?"

"Yeah. The two properties up here, an apartment in London, another in Ibiza, as well as all the cars. Course, she doesn't get a penny if she's guilty."

As Cooper and Tennessee approached the house they were greeted by whom Cooper presumed was Lily Blackburn. Luckily for her, she didn't inherit her father's looks or build, but she did have a strong Blackburn jawline and their trademark dark brown, almost black hair. Lily was reading in the courtyard; she looked elegant in a long-sleeved silk shirt and flowing trousers. Cooper suspected that behind her oversized sunglasses, were the blood-shot eyes of a young woman who'd just lost her father.

"Who are you?" asked the dark-haired woman.

"Lily?"

She nodded reluctantly.

"I'm DCI Cooper, Lily. This is DS Daniel." She nodded at Lily's book. "Reading anything good?"

Lily shook her head. "No. Well, maybe. I can't concentrate on it. Just trying to keep my mind busy." She closed the book and laid it on a patio table. "Where's Charlene?"

The door to the house opened and two men approached the detectives. They were both tall, six-foot or thereabouts, but that was where the similarities ended. The slimmer of the two had medium brown curls and wore round glasses. He moved awkwardly, shading his eyes from the sunlight and looking to the other man to take the lead. The broader man had an august build and hands that looked like wrecking balls. His facial features were misshapen, and hair the colour of black coffee was cropped close to a deformed skull. From what she had heard, Cooper assumed the broader man to be Dylan, Fletcher's eldest, and the slimmer man to be George, the middle child.

She introduced herself, then said, "I'm very sorry for your loss."

George snorted and took a seat next to Lily, who repeated herself. "I asked where Charlene was."

"We're detaining her for now," Cooper said.

George's forehead creased. "You don't think she did it?"

Dylan plodded towards his siblings. "That gold-digging bitch? She's guilty as sin. Of course she did it."

Cooper watched Lily watching Dylan. Even behind the shades, she could tell she wasn't taking her eyes off her older brother.

"Charlene wouldn't kill Dad," George said. "She doesn't have it in her. She's... sweet."

"You would say that," growled Dylan, his body casting a shadow over his siblings.

"Yeah, mummy's boy," Lily added, a teasing tone to her voice. "But," she turned to Cooper, "Charlene's no gold digger. She earned a fortune in her old job." She got to her feet. "I fancy a glass of anything that'll take the edge off. George?"

George nodded and followed his sister. Dylan's jaw tensed. "I'm guessing you're here to speak to me?" he asked. He placed a giant hand on the back of a chair and gripped it, his knuckles changing colour. Cooper had to crane her head upwards. She didn't want to appear intimidated, so she picked up a cushion from where Lily had been sat, fluffed it, then took her seat. Dylan's head was asymmetrical; his skull sloped down sharply on the right-hand side, and his right eye socket sat slightly lower than his left.

"I understand my colleagues questioned you at Morshaw Manor yesterday. But given the circumstances, I'd like to go over things again." Cooper pulled a notepad from her jacket pocket and clicked the top of a pen. "In case you've remembered anything else or want to add anything to your statement."

"You mean if I want to confess to killing my dad?"

"If you did, then confessing would make our lives a lot easier," Cooper said.

"And why would I want to make your lives easier?" Dylan half smiled and took a seat opposite Cooper. "Go on then, ask away."

Cooper steadied herself. There was such darkness and anger in his eyes. The man looked like a cobra that could strike at any moment. "Dylan, you told Sergeant Coombes that you were at home when your father was killed."

"That's right. I was asleep upstairs. I'd been in bed most of the day."

Cooper was sceptical but tried to keep her face neutral. "You slept through four gunshots?"

Dylan shrugged and pointed to the right side of his head. "Deaf in one ear. Have been since birth.

I had an earplug in the other one and had taken some pretty lethal sleeping pills."

"Why did you spend the day in bed?" Tennessee asked.

"I was ill. Migraine attack. Had them all my life. Pain killers do fuck all, so I just knock myself out with sleeping pills and hope that when I wake up it's all over."

"I use sleeping pills from time to time," Tennessee added. "The sound of my six-month-old crying can wake me. I'd think gunshots would still wake most people."

Dylan gave Tennessee a searching look and sized him up. "I'm not most people. Nowt wakes me when I've had those pills. I'm like a tranquillised rhino. Besides, where we live, we're surrounded by woods and farmland. The woods are full of deer, rabbits, pheasants... And there's a clay pigeon range not far away. Our cousin, Theo, used to go. You often hear shotguns going off. It's nowt unusual." He paused before adding a rather sinister, "Someone's always shooting something."

"What time did you take to your bed?" Cooper asked.

"Quite early. Eleven maybe. Probably earlier. Half ten? I woke up at seven that evening with major stomach cramps. Had epic shits."

Cooper did her best not to grimace. He'd probably said it to see her reaction; she didn't give him the satisfaction.

"Probably sat on the bog for over forty minutes." He shifted his ample frame and puffed his chest out. "Then I heard Lily and the gold digger screaming. Brought my headache back in an instant."

"Then what?"

"Went downstairs and found them wailing and covered in blood. Looked around and I saw why."

"And what happened earlier that day? Your father's diary said there was a family meeting."

"Aye. George went over the accounts for this quarter. He's the numbers guy. Dad's talking... or rather he *was* talking, about opening up another two branches of *Gustoso Gustoso*. I imagine that'll fall by the wayside now."

"Who else was there?"

"Just me, Dad, George and Theo."

"Did your father seem different?" Cooper asked.

Dylan thought for a moment. "Nah. He was the same grumpy bastard he always was."

"Not worried about anything, or more stressed than usual?"

Dylan chewed on the end of his thumbnail. "If he was, I didn't notice."

Tennessee raised his hand to his forehead to shade his eyes from the sunlight. "And after the meeting?" he asked.

"I was supposed to do my collections—" He cut himself off.

Tennessee dropped his hand and squinted. "What were you collecting?"

"Just what we were owed."

"Protection money?" Tennessee tried.

"No."

"Loan repayments?"

"No." Dylan rose to his feet. Cooper didn't want the DS to push him too far, so she stepped in, softening her voice in the process.

"Dylan, we know what your father did and why you might want to keep things to yourself, but you don't have to protect him from us. We just want to find out who's responsible for his death."

Dylan didn't sit back down, but he didn't walk away either. "Look, some bars owed us money. I don't know why. It's not my job to know why. It's my job to ask for the money and to get a little heavy-handed if they don't pay up."

Cooper gave him a slight smile, enough to let him know he'd done the right thing in opening up to her, not enough for him to think of her as a friendly little girl. "But you couldn't do your collections because the migraine had started?"

"Dad was pissed. I mean proper veins pulsating at the temples pissed. He grabbed me by the throat and called me a fucking lazy retard."

"I'm sorry," Cooper said as she started to build a picture of Fletcher Blackburn before his death. She was surprised anyone had the balls to grab the beast who sat in front of her by the neck. But if anyone did, it would be another Blackburn.

Dylan huffed. "Don't be. I'm used to it. Been called far worse than that before."

"Your father was a violent man?"

"My father was Fletcher fucking Blackburn. You do the math. So, yeah, I was meant to go into Newcastle, but I can't drive when my head's splitting like that. I can't see properly. I get these visual disturbances, grey patches and flashing lights. Dad said he and Mo would go because, let's face it, George isn't going to get money out of anyone."

"Couldn't someone else have gone? Surely your father had a lot of people working for him?"

Dylan licked his teeth. "It was a bit late notice. The crews have their own business to attend to, and Dad didn't trust the youngsters much. He thought they we are much use as tits on a nun. Besides, he kept a precise schedule when it came to money. If he said Monday morning, someone had to be there to collect on Monday morning. Can't let people think we don't collect a debt when it's due."

"What about Theo? Could he have gone?"

"He'd already left by then, and he wasn't picking up." His shoulders rose and fell. "What can I say? Dad was an *if you want owt done properly, do it yourself* sort of man."

Cooper made a note. She wanted to know if Theo was the sort of person who'd be welcome at Morshaw and therefore get inside without Mo intervening. She also wanted to know where he'd been if he hadn't been answering his phone that morning. "Were Theo and your father close?"

"Yeah, I'd say so. With Eddie doing time I think dad sort of adopted Theo. Not that he needed it. He's old enough and ugly enough to look after himself."

"Did he come to Morshaw often?"

Dylan considered the question. "Few times a week. Family meetings, the odd dinner..." He sucked his lips in, reluctant to add anything further.

"If you can give me a list of the bars you were due to visit, Dylan, it would be really useful. It might help us track down anyone your father encountered that day."

He seemed in two minds, shifting his weight and folding and unfolding his arms. "Fuck it. There's eight of 'em."

Cooper's pen hovered over her notepad.

"Feisty's, McDermott's, LOL, The Silver Mirror, erm... Stilettos, Vixen, Bambi Bar and Bubbles."

Cooper hadn't heard of half of them. "Bubbles?"

"Yeah. They have a bubble machine," he said flatly. "Have foam parties. That sort of shit."

"Are these all in Newcastle city centre?"

"Aye. Most of them are in Grainger Town; the others are over near the station."

"Thanks, Dylan," Cooper said. "Two final things. Have you seen this gun before?" She handed him a photograph of the gun found in Charlene's drawer."

Dylan barely glanced at the photo. "No."

"Please look again."

His jaw clenched before he grudgingly turned his eyes back to the picture of the gun. "Was this the one used to shoot Dad?"

Cooper confirmed that it was.

"Don't recognise it."

She didn't believe him. His body language was giving off multiple signals that he was concealing something. He chewed his jaw, his arms twitched, he shifted his weight.

"Okay, Dylan, last question for now. Did anyone check on you after you went to bed? Or did anyone other than your father and Mo know that you'd taken ill?"

"You want to know if anyone can corroborate my story?" He filled his lungs, expanding his already impressive chest and clenched his hands in boulder-like fists. "Listen, love—"

Cooper squirmed, not from his use of *love*, but from the menacing stare he was directing straight at her.

"If I'd wanted to kill my father... I wouldn't need a fucking gun to do it. Do I look like I need a gun?"

- Chapter 8 -

DS Paula Keaton snorted at DC Oliver Martin. He had a light dusting of icing sugar over the tip of his nose and most of his chin. She couldn't decide if he looked more like a baby covered in talcum powder or a lawyer covered in cocaine. She picked up a napkin from the table of the mom and pop café they were in and dabbed at his face.

"Stop squirming," she said.

"Stop babying me."

It was a quaint little place with checkered tablecloths and copper kettles, bone china and cheese scones the size of cantaloupe melons. A woman in her early sixties took a photo of her scone and said something to her husband about a blog. "Not as good as Penshaw Butchers, better than Cresswell. I'd give it an eight and a half out of ten."

Everyone needs a hobby, Keaton thought, then she wiped the last of the icing sugar from Martin's chin.

"The food's supposed to go in your mouth, not all over your face. The sooner you learn that, the sooner I can stop cleaning up after you."

Martin swiped her hand away. "Pack it in. Look." He nodded to a grand house opposite the café, where a pair of icy-blue, his-and-hers Audis were pulling up the driveway. A stout man in a designer suit emerged from the bigger car, and a slender woman in a teal dress, clutching a teddy bear and a basket of fruit, emerged from the smaller one. The man pulled the woman to him and kissed the top of her head. He lowered himself to whisper something in her ear before guiding her to the front door.

Martin mumbled, "Finally," and got to his feet, only to be yanked back into his seat by Keaton.

"Hold your horses."

"What? The Hansons are home. Let's go talk to them."

Keaton shook her head. "Patience, Grasshopper. Tell me what you see."

Martin frowned and ran a hand through his dark, gelled hair. The residual icing sugar on his fingers left a white streak. Keaton considered telling him, but it was more fun to leave him be. Besides, he looked like a badger. It was cute.

"Okay, okay. What do I see? I see high-end cars with custom alloys, a well maintained front garden, the exterior of the house looks like it's recently been painted and their wheelie bins are hidden behind bamboo screens. I'd say the Hansons like to keep up appearances. They're wealthy without being tacky, and they don't mind everyone knowing it."

Keaton smiled. "Good. What else?"

"They're security conscious. There's no ghastly gate at the end of the drive, but there're sensors and motion-activated lights. They have shutters on the windows, and I heard a bark when they opened the door."

"Sounded like a Dobermann," Keaton added.

Martin's eyes fixed on her. "You can identify a dog breed by its bark?" he asked incredulously.

"You mean you can't?" Keaton teased. She stood and paid their bill, grinning to herself and wondering how Martin hadn't spotted the window decal on Mrs Hanson's car for Dobermann Rescue UK.

The pair left the café with its sweet smell of freshly baked goods, crossed the road and walked up the driveway to the Hanson home. It was a beautiful home in a place called Rowlands Gill. Situated in Gateshead's green belt, the village had once been part of Country Durham but joined Tyne and Wear in the seventies. It was a picturesque spot famous for red kites and being the home of one of the Hairy Bikers, though Keaton could never remember which one. A house like Hanson's, in a village such as this, was the sort of place Keaton wished to have one day. Peaceful. Away from the hubbub of the city and the busier neighbourhoods, but still within an easy commute of HQ. April would like it too, she thought, thinking of her partner. Plenty of room for her blasted cats.

The door swung open before Martin could even knock. One of the sensors must have alerted Hanson to their approach.

"Christ. What do you lot want?" Wayne Hanson asked. Up close, his hair was flecked with grey, and he had innumerable wrinkles around his eyes. Probably from giving so many of his lackeys threatening looks over the years.

"I think you know," Keaton said, holding up her ID. There was a deafening series of barks and the rumbling of weighty dog paws from somewhere behind Hanson. Keaton took a step back and felt for the retractable baton she carried.

"Sit, Gazza. SIT!" Hanson's command brought the stampeding Dobermann to a standstill. It lowered its bottom to the floor and waited for further instructions. "Bloody Blackburns. Nothing but trouble. From behind bars, from beyond the fucking grave... Bloody trouble. Right, best you come in. Don't pet the dog."

Keaton gave the dog a wide berth as she and Martin followed Hanson. Gazza had a docked tail, clipped ears and a shifty look in his eye. Whilst he looked to weigh half of what Keaton did, she didn't fancy her chances.

"Put the kettle on, Traci," Hanson boomed through an open door before turning back to the detectives. "Right, let's have it then. And before you start, the dog looked like that when we adopted him. Cutting an innocent animal's ears off? Barbaric is what it is. Illegal for a reason. His previous owners should have been hung drawn and quartered."

Keaton had read everything she could find on Hanson. When he was thirteen, he served three years in a YOI for taking a knife to a classmate's ear. It appeared his hatred of mutilation didn't extend to his fellow humans.

Hanson's living room was surprisingly chintzy with floral prints on the walls and upholstery. Above a wide fireplace, a family portrait hung showing Hanson and Traci with whom Keaton presumed were his mother and three children. Two older boys and a much younger girl. A jade-coloured urn sat on the mantlepiece. It was labelled *Mam*. In the corner of the room stood an impressive globe in sepia colours. Keaton suspected it opened up into a liquor cabinet.

"Mr Hanson, I'd like to ask you about your relationship with Fletcher Blackburn."

"What relationship?"

Here we go. "How do you know each other?"

Hanson sat down on his floral sofa. "Who says I know him?"

Keaton could feel her hormone levels rising. "Don't treat me like an idiot, Mr Hanson. You know why we called. Fletcher Blackburn and Ibrahim Moradi were shot dead, and you were one of the last people to meet with them."

Hanson took a slow breath before calmly answering. "We're just golf buddies. That's all."

Keaton tilted her head to the side and eyeballed Hanson. "Aye. And I'm a SlimFast shake away from being a supermodel. Let's start with your meeting with him on Sunday and don't fob me off, it's listed in Fletcher's diary, and they have you on camera turning up at Morshaw."

Something changed in Hanson's posture. The camera footage had been wiped from Monday morning onwards, but Hanson would only know that if he'd been the one to erase it. Had he intended to wipe the footage from earlier on? He said nothing.

Martin cleared his throat. "Mr Hanson," he said in a much more soothing tone than the one Keaton had been using. "We don't work for the National Crime Agency. We work for CID. We investigate murders, rapes, assaults and armed robberies. We only want to solve the murders of Fletcher Blackburn and Ibrahim Moradi. I promise you, how you make a living is of no interest to me. Help us to rule you out."

Hanson clearly appreciated the softly, softly approach because he relaxed further into his sofa. The rattling of teacups on saucers preceded Traci Hanson's arrival. She walked into the room with dainty steps and placed a silver tray of tea and biscuits on a side table. She avoided looking at anyone, including her husband, then retreated again. Keaton clocked her red eyes and bitten fingernails.

"Okay," Hanson conceded. "I met Fletcher on Sunday."

Martin sighed. "Thank you. I'm curious why the meeting was at Morshaw. I was under the impression that family were the only ones allowed in Fletcher's home."

He shrugged. "Kings recognise kings."

"So, it's a respect thing?" Martin asked. "As heads of powerful families, you're expected to show hospitality to one another?"

"That's right."

Damn, Martin was doing well. Whether Hanson didn't appreciate her manner, or he simply didn't appreciate being asked questions by a woman, it didn't matter. Martin had stepped in at the ideal time with the perfect attitude.

Martin handed Hanson his cup of tea, and Hanson pointed at a box on top of the mantlepiece. "Hand me that, would you?"

If Martin was put out, he hid it well, handing Hanson the box with a smile. Hanson opened the box, pulled out a cigar, cut the tip and lit it.

"We won't be much longer, Mr Hanson. I'd like to know why you met with Fletcher two days in a row? What brought you back yesterday?"

A plume of smoke formed in front of Hanson's face, then it dissipated into a wispy line of white. "I didn't meet him yesterday."

"His diary says you did." Keaton countered.

"His diary's wrong. We met on Sunday."

There was another puff of smoke. Keaton hated the smell, it was going to seep into her clothes and her hair. She'd taste it on every bite of food she'd have that day. As an athlete, her lung capacity had been legendary. She never tired, never faded. The thought of that poison filtering into her lungs made her want to pull her shirt up around her mouth and form a makeshift mask.

"I was busy yesterday. All day."

"Where were you?" Martin asked.

"The hospital. Been there most of this morning too. My little girl's sick. Measles."

"I'm sorry to hear that," Martin said while Keaton made a note.

"Which hospital?" she asked.

"The RVI," Hanson answered. "She'll pull through. She's tough. She's a Hanson." He pointed to the family portrait. "Millie. My baby girl."

Martin hesitated then asked, "Why did you meet with Fletcher on Sunday?"

"You know I'm not going to incriminate myself, boy."

"Come on, Wayne."

Nice touch, thought Keaton. Switching to his first name after all that sycophancy. It caught Hanson off guard.

"I don't want to bring you in. My colleague here would love to drag you to HQ and parade you in front of the press as our number one suspect, but I don't want that. I also don't want to have to do a Capone and start sifting through every tax return you've ever submitted."

"But you will?" Hanson growled with narrow eyes.

Martin leant closer. "Help me help you."

He groaned and puffed on the cigar again. "Let me put it this way. We have a joint venture. Or we did. The enemy of my enemy is my friend. That sort of thing."

"Who's the shared enemy?" Martin asked.

Martin was met with silence while Hanson mulled over whether he should answer or not. Martin didn't press him; instead, he picked up two biscuits and handed one to Keaton. They nibbled away while they waited.

"The Roker Boys," he finally answered. "Bloody Mackems getting too big for their boots. Neither us nor the Blackburns can take them down on our own."

The word *Mackem* is a nickname given to people from the City of Sunderland. Where Newcastle and Gateshead are severed by the River Tyne, it's the Wear that flows through Sunderland. Tynesiders and Wearsiders, whilst neighbours, had always been rivals.

Martin asked the obvious question. "But together you could?"

"Exactly. The plan was to out muscle them. Then the Blackburns would have Roker, Fulwell and Southwick. I'd manage Pallion, Thornhill and Hendon."

Martin caught Keaton's eye. They were thinking the same thing. If the Roker Boys had got wind of Fletcher's intentions, they wouldn't have hesitated in protecting their interests. Had someone blabbed?

- Chapter 9 -

It took the best part of half an hour for Cooper and Tennessee to walk back from Bamburgh to the Blackburns' barn conversion in Budle Bay. In the interests of their health, they'd opted to leave the car and take a leisurely stroll to a restaurant called The Potted Lobster. They'd been lucky to get a seat; the sunshine had brought the hikers and the twitchers in droves. Cooper found a small table in the corner and they ordered two bowls of mussels with crusty bread and shared a portion of truffle and parmesan fries.

With full bellies, they tackled the walk back along a country road that was lined with thickets and nettles. Lacking a pavement, they occasionally had to dodge traffic and walk on the grass verge. Cooper walked barefoot, carrying her heeled shoes. The road was smooth and warm, having been heated by the midday sun. Every hundred metres or so Cooper would turn her head and look back towards Bamburgh to see if she could still see the castle looming in the distance. She could. Now and again they would pass a gate between bushes and could look in on fields of oblivious sheep and nosy cows.

Tennessee passed the time by trying to convince Cooper that she should sign up to a charity relay triathlon that the commissioner had organised in a bid to boost public relations. Northumbria Police versus the Tyne and Wear Fire Service. Cooper was less than enthusiastic. For one, Tennessee had bagsied the cycling leg and Keaton, as the former professional full-back, had been nominated to do the running leg. That would leave Cooper with the open-water swim. In the North Sea? No, thank you. Secondly, she could see it now. For every member of the public cheering them on there'd be some-one jeering that they should bloody get back to work.

Both Cooper and Tennessee were rosy-cheeked when they arrived back at the barn, hoping to speak to Lily Blackburn. They found Lily propping up the kitchen island with a glass of something sparkling in her hand.

"To Dad," she said, toasting the air. "Hope you don't mind, but I thought I'd get the weekend start-ed early.

Cooper didn't want to judge; the girl had just lost her father. But she was thrown by Lily's choice to wear sunglasses indoors because as far as Cooper was aware, only two types of people wore sunglass-es indoors: the blind, and celebrity arseholes.

"As you're aware, Lily, we have your step-mother in custody—"

"Urgh. Don't call her my step-mother: she's Charlene. And George is right, she wouldn't hurt Dad. Besides, she was out with me. You should have seen her when we found... when we found them." Lily paused, her lower lip quivering. "She was beside herself. When are you going to let her come home?"

"As soon as we can establish if she handled the gun that killed your father," Cooper said. "What I was wondering, was how your mother felt about your father's marriage to Charlene?"

Lily shook her head and let out a shallow laugh. "If you mean, did she approve, then no, of course not. Charlene's only five years older than me. When I was born, she was still learning to use a knife and fork."

"So, she's more like a big sister?" Tennessee asked.

"Urgh," she grunted again. "Yeah. Maybe. If you say so. Sometimes we were close, but it was weird. I mean, she was Dad's wife."

Cooper looked to a pair of bar stools next to the marble-topped island. "May we?"

Lily shrugged, so they took their seats. Cooper looked down and saw that Tennessee's feet rested on the floor, whereas hers dangled a good six inches away. She felt like a child taking a seat at the big table.

"I know Ibrahim was well-regarded by your father. Would he allow your mother into Morshaw?"

"Oh, no. Not at all," Lily said, shaking her head. "She tried once: a year after the divorce. She was drunk as a skunk and driving this way and that, yelling through the intercom... Anyway, Mo let the dogs out, so she took off."

"And your mother lives in Turkey?" Cooper asked.

"Last I heard. She hasn't answered my calls since all this happened. I don't know if she's even heard yet."

Cooper gave Tennessee a look. They'd developed a good level of telepathy over the years, so she didn't have to glance at his notepad to know that he was writing, *check H. Blackburn is not in the country.*

"Who is allowed through the gates?" Cooper continued.

"Well... family, obviously. Me and the boys. Charlene, Theo—"

"That's Eddie's son?"

"Yeah." She wet her lower lip and took a sip of Champagne. "Then there's Pilates Paulo. You know about him?"

Cooper confirmed that she did.

"We have a chef on weekends too. He cooks for Dad and Charlene on Saturday nights. It's like their date night thing." She pulled a face. "Then he stays in the guest room and makes breakfast and lunch for us the next day. Dad likes us to eat Sunday lunch together as a family."

"That sounds nice," Cooper said.

Lily's mouth curled down. "It can be. Depends on what mood Dad and Dylan are in. And it's not like Dad had much of an appetite lately; he was pretty much on a liquid diet. Gross health drinks in the morning and whiskey in the afternoon. I suppose you'll want the chef's details?"

Cooper nodded. Lily jotted down a name and handed it to her: *Darren Ray*. She finished her glass and stifled a burp before opening the fridge and getting herself a top-up.

"Charlene mentioned you don't have a cleaner."

"No. Apparently, that's a woman's job." She closed the fridge and swayed slightly. "I know Charlene doesn't mind cleaning. I mean, it's not like she was busy doing much else, other than riding Dad or working on her tan. But I work. I have no intention of cleaning up after the men all day. It's a tad 1950s."

"What do you do?" Tennessee asked.

"I work in a beautician's. Nails, waxing, that sort of thing. I'm still learning the basics, but I plan on running my own salon one day. Maybe a boutique too. I'm into fashion, and I have an online presence. I'm a bit of an influencer. I get sent stuff to promote." She tapped the side of her designer shades.

Okay, Cooper thought. Three types of people wear sunglasses indoors: the blind, celebrity arseholes, and wannabe celebrity arseholes.

"Nice," Tennessee said when Cooper failed to respond. "And I'm sorry to ask. But can you tell us where you were on Monday?"

"I was out with Charlene. We went to Doxford for dinner and massages. We've already been over this?"

"Yes, but I meant earlier in the day."

Lily sighed. "I'm getting tired, and there are arrangements to be made... I haven't slept." A tear rolled down her cheek, and she turned away to dab under her glasses with a sheet of kitchen roll. "But fine, I was at home until ten, maybe quarter past, then I went into work for a few hours." She steadied her voice and turned back to face them. "And between clients, I got my nails done, curled my eyelashes and got everything waxed," she paused to look at Tennessee. "Everything."

THE RIOT IN HMP Frankland began at eight p.m. precisely, just as he'd asked. The guards and their riot shields struggled against the sea of men holding them back. One-on-one with a guard was an impossibility; they had shields, sprays, batons and dogs. But like ants, when the inmates worked as a team, they could achieve great things, and right now, they were holding off twenty guards. In the distance, Eddie Blackburn could hear the German shepherds preparing for battle. The faintest barks over the constant drone of sirens.

Like a king surveying his lands from a mountain citadel, Eddie Blackburn watched the chaos unfold. Heath held the man still while Blackjack jammed the shank into his ribs three times. He was their second target; the first lay dying under a pile of plastic chairs. The man crumpled to the floor only to be trodden on in the stampede of approaching inmates. J-wing had heeded the call and were coming to join in the fun. Blackjack hauled the man out of the chaos, grabbed his left arm and pulled it violently, dislocating it at the shoulder. He screamed and raised his right arm to defend himself, only to have his elbow kicked—and probably broken—by Heath. Blood pooled around him, and he begged for his life like a child begs not to go to bed early.

Eddie never took kindly to begging: it only made him angrier.

Blackjack cleared some space. "He's all yours, Eddie."

Eddie approached slowly. He was in no hurry. He could watch the riot all night; it was likely to last that long anyway, and it was the best entertainment he'd had in a long time.

The man was crying, sobbing even. "Please. Please, Eddie. You don't have to do this. It wasn't me, you know it wasn't."

Eddie bent over him and lowered his lips to his ear. "I know it wasn't, but this is war," he whispered. "Wars have casualties."

The man bucked and flinched. "No. Eddie. No." His arms were useless, flopping by his sides, unable to protect him.

Eddie dragged the tip of the shank over the lens of his eyeball. The man screamed, but his sounds barely carried over the noise of mayhem.

Eddie grinned. "An eye for an eye."

The shank plunged through the iris and into the vitreous body. The scream that followed was one Eddie would never forget. He pulled the shank free and admired the eyeball impaled on the end of it. He wanted to keep it as a trophy but knew no good would come from that, so he pulled it free and let it roll through the bedlam until it was trampled by Fat Matt from G-wing.

Eddie walked back to his cell and stood in his doorway. The citadel that was his cell was calm and secure. All he had to do was close the door behind him. He took one last look at his soldiers as they did his bidding then returned to his bed. It felt good to be the king.

- Chapter 10 -

Forensic pathologist Margot Swanson finished her pre-work cigarette while strolling around the small lake in Paddy Freeman's park. She savoured this moment each day; it was her *above-ground time*. Margot kept this routine regardless of the weather. Still, she especially liked days like today when the sun was bright, the sky was blue, and the green heads of the mallards on the lake shimmered in the sunlight. She stubbed out her cigarette at the bin near the entrance to the park then headed into the Freeman to start her shift. Margot nipped to the ladies room, swilled with mouthwash and moisturised her hands. She didn't like to look at her hands, so she kept her eyes on the reflection in the mirror. Dermatitis and age had ravaged the backs of her fingers. She could colour her roots, get fillers every six months and keep as much pep in her step as she could manage, but her hands would always give her away.

"Relax," she purred to her reflection. "You're only as old as the man you feel... and Tony's twenty-six."

She smiled as she thought of the athletic young man to whom she was engaged. She hadn't expected them to last: they rarely did. The novelty usually wore off after a couple of months, and one or both of them would move onto pastures new. This one had been different. He'd seen past her age, and she'd seen past his youth. They connected. It sounded like such soppy tripe, but the words *soulmates* kept coming to mind. Margot rubbed the inner edge of her engagement ring with her thumb and headed back to the morgue, keeping thoughts of dissection at bay with thoughts of being cuddled up on the sofa with the man she'd fallen for. She fancied watching a film tonight. Something spooky so they could cuddle even tighter during the scary bits.

The morgue in the bowels of the Freeman was sterile and chilly, with white and avocado-green tiles that reminded Margot of her parent's bathroom where she'd grown up in Elgin. Margot covered her lab coat with a transparent apron with sleeves and got to work. She'd finished the autopsy of Ibrahim Moradi last night and was ready to get to know Fletcher Blackburn. His body was wheeled from storage and his ankle barcode scanned. Margot opened the file she'd received from radiology and examined the x-rays that had been taken on intake. The x-rays showed two old breaks, the first was to the left radius and the second to the right tibia. According to his medical history, these both occurred when Fletcher was in his late teens.

The radial break was from fighting with his older brother, and the tibial break occurred after he jumped out of a tree. A bright oval of white, clearly visible in the x-ray, indicated a bullet remained in the body.

"Good morning, Fletcher."

Admittedly, it was an odd custom to greet the dead, but it was a custom Margot had continued from her old mentor at the University of Edinburgh.

"Let's get you more comfortable," she said as she began to undress the body. Some pathologists were rushed and handled DBs like rag dolls. Margot preferred a slower, more respectful manner. Fletcher's shirt, suit jacket and trousers were removed, folded, bagged and sealed as evidence. She didn't like to cut clothing unless absolutely necessary. His wallet, keys and watch were placed to one side for his next of kin. As she did this, Margot paused to think of the family and the grief they would be experiencing. The cold, naked body that lay before her was once a living, breathing human, and he was worthy of being handled with dignity.

"Fletcher Blackburn, fifty-two," she said, pressing record on a dictaphone. "Wednesday nineteenth of June, ten-forty a.m. Commencing anterior external examination... Loose skin on the arms and abdomen suggests recent weight loss. Slight jaundice to the eyes and skin. Two entrance wounds consistent with gunshots to the torso. One appears to be through the fourth rib on the left-hand side, just proximal to the costal cartilage. The second wound is through the sixth rib on the right-hand side. There are bruises to the right shin."

Margot applied an ink roller to Fletcher's fingertips and pressed each finger in turn against a piece of card. She then collected samples from under his nails and gently rolled the body over. "Posterior external examination reveals an exit wound to the left of the lumbar spine," she said before turning Fletcher back. She took a scalpel and made a Y-shaped incision from his shoulders to his sternum and down to the groin. "Exposing the ribs confirms the location of the wounds to left four and right six."

Margot's next job was to remove the front of the ribcage to give her access to the organs. To do this, she needed rib cutters: pruning sheers for the human body. She removed the lungs, photographed the position of the remaining bullet, retrieved it and bagged it for the investigating team. Next, she weighed the lungs and took samples of lung tissue. She collected samples of urine, blood and bile, labelled the vials and put them to one side for analysis.

Removing the stomach to examine its contents was one of the worse aspects of her work, and never a task Margot enjoyed. She weighed the stomach, braced herself and made her incision.

Margot paused and lowered her head to get a closer look. She picked up some pieces of purple and green with a pair of tweezers and held them up to the light.

"Well," she said, removing her gloves and picking up the morgue's telephone. "This just got interesting."

- Chapter 11 -

Yesterday had been one hellish long day. Cooper had returned home in the early evening to find her home abandoned save for the baby seagull that was now living in her kitchen. Steven Seagull had outgrown his shoebox and was now housed in a straw-filled crate that sat in the corner of the room between the bin and the fridge. Cooper's first task of the evening was to disinfect the kitchen floor because try as she might, Tina hadn't been able to toilet train the winged beast. Her second task was to text Tina and find her whereabouts. Her fifteen-year-old was having dinner at her boyfriend's and promised to be home before dark. True to form, Tina arrived two minutes before the official sunset time. Cooper threw a ready meal in the microwave and ate it straight from its plastic tray.

As night fell, Cooper did everything she could to give herself the best chance of a good night's sleep. She showered, applied lavender body lotion, drank camomile tea and played relaxing music as she pulled on some pyjamas. After the events of April, Cooper was never sleeping naked again. She curled up and tried to create an environment of sensory deprivation by using earplugs and an eye mask. Unfortunately, the earplugs couldn't block out her thoughts, and her mind continuously circled back to Atkinson and his glamorous bloodstain analyst. They were no doubt sharing a delicious bottle of red while they discussed all things forensics. The regret and jealousy that raged inside her kept Cooper awake until four a.m., which is why, when she arrived at CID, she looked like morning breath personified.

Cooper had barely crossed the threshold when Chief Superintendent Howard Nixon summoned her to his office.

"Don't sit. This won't take long."

Cooper stood awkwardly and wished she'd stopped for coffee on her way in. Facing Howard Nixon while in a decaffeinated state was never a wise move.

"Andre Spence and Charlie Mellor. Those names mean anything to you, Cooper?"

"Should they?" Cooper looked Nixon up and down. He was well dressed, as always, but his skin was oddly pale for this time of year, and his greying hair was thinning at the temples. He was stressed.

"They're two of Wayne Hanson's crew. Murdered last night during a riot at Frankland."

Cooper's shoulders sagged as she considered the implications. "Shit."

"Shit? Shit doesn't begin to cover it. Spence was hit on the back of the head, his eyeballs removed, then stabbed multiple times. Mellor had both arms broken, eyeballs removed then stabbed and kicked to death."

Cooper felt faint. She could actually feel the blood draining from her head and had to place a hand on Nixon's doorway to make sure she didn't collapse. "*An eye for an eye?* Bloody hell. Sir, last I heard from Keaton, she didn't think Hanson had anything to do with this. I don't have all the details yet, but she said the Hansons and the Blackburns were working together on something."

"Didn't anyone tell Eddie this?"

"Probably, sir. He must have thought they'd been stabbed in the back. We're going to have a war on our hands."

"Blackburn, Moradi, Spence and Mellor. That's four." He held up four fingers on his right hand to force home the point. "I'd say the war has already started. Wouldn't you?"

"Yes, sir."

He gestured towards the door, but Cooper needed something first. Once she was sure her legs wouldn't give way, she told Nixon what she needed. "As you know, sir, we have Charlene Blackburn in custody. The gun was found in her underwear draw. We're still following up on her alibi, but I haven't heard back from the lab yet. I'm hoping they'll find a print or some DNA on the gun that can tie this to Charlene but our twenty-four hours are almost up. I need an extension if I'm to hold her any longer."

Nixon nodded and turned his attention back to his computer monitor. He didn't have to say anything; the extension to thirty-six hours would be approved.

"COFFEE?"

DS Paula Keaton was a mind reader. She held a cardboard tray containing four steaming cuppas in one hand and carried three ring binders in the other. Cooper took one of the coffees and headed to a table in the corner of CID where Tennessee and Martin were sat. She'd just got off the phone with her mother. They didn't speak often, but that didn't mean there was any bad blood. Her parents were living their lifelong dream of running a bar in the sunshine. Benji's Bar catered to the British and Irish crowd. During the summer the place was packed with tourists and brought in the big bucks, but it was the quieter winter months that Julie and Ben Cooper enjoyed the most, when the local ex-pat community gathered in the bar and swapped stories about the previous season. Cooper and Tina tried to visit every other year, and they always received a warm welcome from the bar's regulars. She wondered how they'd react to her new hair—or lack of it—when she and Tina made the journey this Christmas. Julie, her mother, had droned on for a good while about her friends, the Smalls, and had told a fifteen-minute story about a taxi driver that didn't seem to go anywhere. The story, not the driver. It was towards the end of the conversation that Julie had mentioned Ben's tight chest and shortness of breath for the past day or so.

"Mum! You need to take him to A&E."

"Always, such a worrier. It will have been that giant surf and turf he ate on Monday. Trust me."

"I trust doctors more."

"Well Dr Diaz will be in later; he's always in on a Wednesday night. I'll have a chat—"

"Mum!" Cooper had to stop herself from snapping at her. "Dr Diaz is an orthopaedic surgeon. You need to speak to a cardiologist. Do it today. Please."

It had taken ten minutes of persuading to convince Julie that it was worth shutting the bar for an afternoon to be sure and to put their daughter's mind at rest. *Family.*

Keaton took a seat next to Cooper. "Tennessee tells me you're up for swimming in the relay triathlon."

"Did he now?" Cooper flashed him a scathing look. "I'd rather scratch my eyes out. Speaking of which, I'm sure you've heard what went down last night?"

They all nodded, looking serious.

"And as for the swim, Martin can do it."

Martin coughed. He was looking even more well-kempt when usual. His shirt had been ironed to within an inch of its life, and he was definitely wearing a new aftershave. "Sorry, boss. I'm already in a team with Boyd and Whyte. We don't stand a chance, but it's for a good cause."

Keaton pressed her palms together in prayer and tried to give Cooper the puppy dog eyes. "Please," she said in a voice that was high-pitched and girlie and didn't suit her one bit. "I neeeeed to compeeeete."

"Urgh. Fine. Just never pull that face again."

Keaton punched the air jubilantly and folded her legs so that her left foot rested on her right knee. Her eyes flicked to the doors as Saffron Boyd and Elliot Whyte arrived. *Great.* Cooper's mind was suddenly in the past, hiding around the side of North Shields Police Station, crying her eyes out and hoping none of her colleagues saw.

Boyd and Whyte took their seats and nodded hellos to the rest of the team. Martin sat up a little straighter and couldn't mask his joy that Boyd had chosen the seat next to him. *That explained the aftershave.* Keaton pointed a finger in Whyte's face and said, "Morning Ell-i-ot," as if she was E.T.

Whyte, though lower in rank, didn't hesitate to swipe her finger away. Martin chuckled and mimicked Keaton's teasing. "Ell-i-ott."

"All right, pack it in," warned Cooper. "We have work to be getting on with. Tennessee, you're up first."

"Right. Fletcher's ex-wife, Hazel, also known as *the witch...*"

Keaton and Martin giggled.

"...is not in Turkey."

"She's not?" Cooper leant in.

"There's no evidence that she's in the UK, but she boarded a flight to Barcelona from Istanbul two and a half weeks ago and hasn't returned yet."

"Date?" Cooper asked.

"Second of June. She's been posting prolifically on social media. Several posts per day to both Facebook and Instagram since at least three days before Fletcher and Ibrahim were murdered. It's almost like—"

"Like she wants the world to see she has an alibi," Cooper finished for him.

"Exactly." Tennessee interlaced his fingers and stretched his arms above his head. "But she messed up." Five sets of eyebrows lifted around the table and he presented a printout from Hazel Blackburn's Facebook page. "This leathery-looking lady is Hazel Blackburn. According to Facebook, she was reclining on this sun lounger with a mojito at quarter past three on Monday afternoon, however, see this little detail?"

"Published by Hootsuite," Cooper read. "What's Hootsuite?"

"It's a social media management platform. It allows users to schedule posts in advance. Hazel could have taken that photo an hour before, or a week before."

Cooper leant back in her seat and savoured her coffee while she mulled things over. "Interesting. Find out what hotel she's supposedly at and give them a call."

The DS nodded.

"Keaton, you're next."

Keaton sat up tall and began to fill the team in on her and Martin's trip to Rowlands Gill to speak with Wayne Hanson.

"Martin managed to get some quality intel out of Hanson. He and Fletcher Blackburn were working together to muscle the Roker Boys out of Sunderland. They were after their territory. He admits to being at Morshaw on Sunday but flat out denies being there on Monday. Say's the diary entry is wrong and that he never saw Fletcher again after their Sunday meeting."

"Alibi?" Cooper asked.

"At the RVI most of the day with his sick daughter. I've spoken to the ward in question and have the names of some of the nurses who were on duty at the time. I'll nip over today and speak to them."

"Good. Tennessee, remind me to check with George Blackburn when we speak to him. See if he knows anything about another meeting.

Tennessee nodded and made a note.

"Okay," Cooper continued. "In case anyone hadn't heard, two of Hanson's crew were killed in Frankland during a riot last night. I'll spare you the gory details, but the photographs are in this file if any of you want to have nightmares. I'm not daft enough to put this down to coincidence. This is Eddie's work. He clearly thinks Hanson's to blame, either by killing Fletcher or by tipping off the Roker Boys."

"Do you think it'll escalate?" Boyd asked in her quiet voice.

"I'd say so," Tennessee answered. "I imagine Hanson will be pissed. He'll probably retaliate. We should probably tail him."

Cooper agreed. "Can't be you two though," She directed at Keaton and Martin. "He'll recognise you, and by now he'll know I'm heading the investigation. I'll have to arrange for—"

"He won't recognise me," Boyd suggested. "Or Elliot."

Whyte dipped his chin and looked to Cooper. My God, she hated his face. It had aged since their time together at North Shields, but his face still represented the way he'd made her feel all those years ago.

"We can tail him," he said. "We've spoken to all the nearest neighbours, and there's absolutely nothing worth following up. We're free to do it."

"All right. Be careful," Cooper said, looking at Boyd in particular, "and keep a good distance."

"What about the Blackburns?" Keaton asked. "Do we offer them protection?"

Tennessee snorted. "Waste tax payer's money protecting vermin? Besides, they can protect themselves."

Cooper was in two minds. She agreed with Tennessee's summation, but she also didn't want any blood on her hands. "One squad car," she said. "We'll post it on the road between their barn conversation and Bamburgh. Close enough to see any comings and goings, not so close that the Blackburns feel suffocated and do a runner somewhere we won't find them. I still want to keep them on side. Which leads me to this situation with the Roker Boys."

"Whether it was Hanson who tipped them off or not," Keaton started, "If they knew, they could well have done this to protect themselves."

Boyd shuffled and lifted a finger. "Erm, boss?"

"Yes?"

"I ran a background check on the private chef Lily told you about. Darren Ray, forty-three, squeaky clean, no record. I checked his website and social media accounts and found he was born and raised in Chester-le-Street. He trained at a catering college in Sunderland before moving to London to work with Marco Pierre White. He stayed there for over ten years, then returned to the northeast to set up his own business." She nibbled at a nail before adding. "He trained in Roker Boy territory. I wondered if he knew them back in the day."

"And that he might do them a favour by knocking off Fletcher?" Cooper finished for her.

She shrugged. "Just a thought."

"It's a good thought," Martin said with a smile. "Coop likes it when we spitball ideas. Don't be scared to share a theory with her." He looked to Cooper.

"Martin's right, and we should keep his name in the mix for now. I don't think Fletcher would be foolish enough to talk business in front of the chef, but there is a small chance the Roker Boys recruited him. It doesn't explain how he got access to Morshaw on a Monday. Lily said he was only there Saturday and Sundays."

"Maybe he left something on purpose so he had the excuse of going back to collect it?" Boyd said in her quiet voice.

Cooper wasn't so sure, but she didn't want to put Boyd off when she was so shy already. "Okay, well you know the drill. Trace, interview, eliminate. If you get anything, great. If not, don't worry. Let's not dwell too long on this though, we don't even know if the Roker Boys knew anything about the Blackburns and the Hansons. It's all speculation right now."

Martin's lips slid back and forth over his teeth as he mulled something over. "It's not like we can even ask the Roker Boys. I mean, imagine it, *Hi Guys, quick question. Did you know the Blackburns and Hansons were teaming up to muscle you off your turf?*"

"Because if they did know, they wouldn't tell us," said Tennessee.

"And if they didn't..." Cooper considered. "Well, we'd have a three-way war on our hands," She gulped down what remained of the coffee and got to her feet. "Tennessee, we have a meeting with forensics. Boyd, Whyte, you two tail Hanson and arrange for the car to monitor the Blackburns. Keaton and Martin, follow up on Hanson's alibi and pay a visit to Cedric in Local Intelligence. Find out all you can on the Roker Boys: the big players, known associates, latest addresses, likely locations."

Keaton nodded at Martin, they pushed their chairs out and stood up. Before leaving, Keaton pulled Cooper's file across the table and flicked through until she found the photographs from Frankland. She gagged. "Oh, Jeez. That's disgusting."

"Don't say I didn't warn you."

- Chapter 12 -

Justin Atkinson and Veronica Rogers both displayed the slow gait and exaggerated yawns of people who had been up past their bedtimes. Despite this, Atkinson still looked his tall, dashing self with a sprinkle of the Milky Bar Kid geek-chic that made him all the more adorable. Veronica, or Ronnie as she preferred to go by, was rosy-cheeked and without a hair out of place.

"Morning," Cooper greeted the pair as they joined her and Tennessee in the meeting room. "How was the talk?" she braved asking.

"Fabulous," Ronnie gushed, shooting a look of admiration in Atkinson's direction. "But dinner was better. Justin took me to Peace and Loaf. Have you been there? I had scallops with rhubarb and sea lettuce. It looked like a work of art, I almost didn't want to ruin it by eating it."

Of course Cooper had been there. She'd been there with Atkinson and had ordered the bloody scallops. Ronnie was right about it being delicious, but Cooper's stomach twisted at the thought of them there together. Had they ate at the lovely table by the kitchen that gave you a view of the highly skilled chefs at work? Had he ordered her the same wine he'd introduced Cooper too?

Pushing jealous thoughts aside, Cooper simply got down to business. "You said you had some updates?"

Atkinson cleared his throat. "Erm, yes. There were no fingerprints on the gun, not even a partial print. No DNA, no nothing. Someone took great care to make sure that gun was clean. They also cleaned the doorknob on the door to the bedroom and wiped clean the handle on the draw where Hong found the gun."

Cooper's shoulders sagged in disappointment. "That wasn't what I'd hoped for."

"I might be able to put a smile on your face," Ronnie said, spreading her glossed lips into a wide smile. She laid a file on the table, opened it and spread crime scene photographs out in a fan shape."

Cooper told herself Ronnie was probably a lovely person and it wasn't her fault she and Atkinson weren't together. Still, she couldn't help the bitchy feeling that bubbled up inside. She needed to get a grip. She was a Detective Chief Inspector after all.

"I'm certain our shooter was hiding under the desk when the second victim entered the room. Justin's team found gunshot residue on the underside of the desk. It's highly unlikely to have got there had the gun been fired above the desk," Ronnie said.

"And we also found trace evidence of gunshot residue on the hands of Dylan, Lily and Charlene," Atkinson added.

Cooper knew from experience that gunshot residue didn't equal guilt. Lily and Charlene were the ones to discover the bodies. They most likely touched the victims to confirm they had died or to try to come to their aid. Residue can travel up to five feet, so anyone who'd touched furniture or surfaces in the vicinity would have been contaminated.

Ronnie singled out two photographs and pushed them across the table. These are relevant to when Fletcher was shot the first time. You can see the damage where the bullet exited the body and hit the edge of the desk. When combined with what Ms Swanson, the forensic pathologist, has told us, I would estimate the bullet was travelling downwards at an angle of one hundred and forty degrees. There are also void marks on the wall behind where the shooter was stood."

Before Cooper could ask for that in plain English, Ronnie added, "Void marks indicate an absence of blood, where the spatter has been blocked by the body of the shooter. When he was shot the second time, Fletcher was on the floor. The bullet remained in the body, again that's backed up by Ms Swanson, and we have expirated bloodstain patterns on the floor where Fletcher coughed up blood before death."

Cooper winced but signalled to Ronnie to keep going.

"The second victim was shot in the chest first. Justin recovered the bullet from the wall." She handed Cooper another photograph. "The angle of the spatter tails is further evidence that the shooter was under the desk when this occurred. The victim slid down the wall, hence these swipe marks. He was then shot in the head, causing these high velocity spatter patterns mixed with brain matter."

Cooper glanced at Tennessee; he was looking a little rough. She frowned at the two forensic experts. All that information was interesting and helped paint a clear mental image of what happened, but she was unsure which part of the gruesome details was supposed to make her smile.

Reading her mind, Atkinson waded in. "Which brings us to our good news." He smiled at Ronnie then turned back to Cooper. "Without Ronnie, I wouldn't have been able to give you anything more specific than the killer was tall. But, Ronnie is an expert in her field, between her angles and formulas and algorithms, she's narrowed the shooter's height down to five-foot-ten to six-foot-two."

Cooper let out a long sigh and looked to Tennessee. He pulled the mug shot that had been taken of Charlene upon her arrest out of the file.

"Five-two," he said.

Cooper slumped and rested her head on the table. "Damn it." She appreciated that having a good estimate of the shooter's height was useful; it would help them narrow the field. Still, given the turf war implications, it would have been easier on everyone if the wife had done it.

- Chapter 13 -

Dylan Blackburn had one of his headaches. He tore into a fresh box of paracetamol and threw the information leaflet in the bin. Two tablets every four hours? As if that dose would even take the edge off. He took three, along with a higher than recommended dose of ibuprofen. He didn't have time for a headache; there was work to be done. Business didn't stop just because his father was dead.

Dylan stalked towards the stairs, briefly stopping to peer into his sister's room. Lily was lying on her bed, her thumbs busily tip-tapping away at her phone.

"I'm going into town," he said when she looked up.

"Bamburgh or Newcastle?"

"Newcastle."

Lily sat up and crossed her legs. She must have applied her make-up with a trowel this morning.

She looked like a fucking drag queen. "You meeting Theo?"

Dylan sniffed. Wouldn't she like to know? "I'll be back later," was all he said.

His sister grabbed a pillow and threw it towards the door, causing it to slam in his face. *Brat*. Precious little Lily. Always annoyed at being sidelined. She didn't know how good she had it. If she'd had to work day in, day out with the likes of his father and his uncle she'd soon change her tune. She didn't understand the sacrifices he'd had to make to keep her safe. He continued downstairs and fished a black bin liner from under the sink. He opened the tumble dryer and stuffed the items into the bag. George was in the living room with his nose in a book. Dylan grunted at him. It was brother speak for: *see you later.*

It took an hour to drive into Newcastle. Dylan parked in the first pay and display spot he came across, pulled the bin liner from the boot of his car and walked until he found a charity shop. He didn't bother greeting the shop assistant; he didn't care for small talk. Instead, he tossed the bin bag in the sheepish man's direction, mumbled, "Donation," and left, heading towards a street named Bigg Market.

The Bigg Market was once an important trading post for the buying and selling of barley on the Great North Road. Now, it was known for its nineties themed bars, dodgy takeaways and fights in the taxi rank. The street made national news when five hundred drunken Newcastle fans rioted after their defeat to Manchester United in the

1999 cup final. Phone boxes were smashed up and trees uprooted. All because one group of overpaid wankers could kick a ball better than another group of overpaid wankers.

Speaking of overpaid wankers... Dylan found Theo five minutes later in a seedy basement bar with topless barmaids.

Theo was a younger version of his father. Tall and powerful with a round face, a hairline that showed the first signs of receding, and dark, shoulder-length hair secured in a ponytail. He walked with a swagger, thought he was smarter than he was, and the way he talked about women fawning over him: he thought he was Jason fucking Momoa. He clocked Dylan as soon as he entered the bar and finished the few inches of lager left in his pint glass. It wasn't even lunchtime.

"It's five o'clock somewhere," he said, reading Dylan's questioning look. He raised two fingers at the barmaid and practically drooled as he watched her pull two more pints. "You know, cuz, if this is too much for you... I can handle business. If you'd rather be at home with your grieving family."

He didn't look like he could handle business. He looked like he was a few slurps away from slurring his speech. Drinking to forget? What was Theo Blackburn's conscience feeling guilty about?

"I think Dad would feel better knowing his assets were being taken care of by immediate family," Theo continued.

Dylan's lip curled. He knew this would happen. With Uncle Eddie behind bars, Theo saw Fletcher's death as his cue to take the throne. He'd always hated playing yes man to Fletcher when he considered himself the rightful heir.

Dylan moved closer to Theo and watched his face stiffen as he tried not to look intimidated by Dylan's malformed appearance. "I don't take orders from you. Until I hear different from Uncle Eddie, and only Uncle Eddie, business continues as usual. I do my collections, and you do... whatever it is you fucking do." He took one sip of his pint and placed the drink back on the bar. It tasted of warm piss. "When's Hurls getting here?"

Theo checked the expensive watch on his wrist, making sure he lifted his shirt sleeve long enough for the barmaid to see he was wearing at least twelve grand of Swiss engineering. "Any minute now. I hope you lighten up before dinner cuz. I don't want your snarling face mean mugging me while I try and enjoy some lovely pasta."

Dylan bristled. "You're coming to the barn for dinner?"

"Lily invited me. Would be rude not to." He leant closer and whispered, "She's making a lasagne."

The smugness on his face was hard to stomach. "You're fucking disgusting," Dylan said as Hurls entered the room with his minder. Why he had that steroid monkey follow him around everywhere, Dylan would never know. Sure, he looked intimidating to those uneducated in combat, but he'd last less than a minute against someone like Dylan.

Paddy Harlow-Hurley preferred to go by Hurls. Double-barrelled names sounded a bit wank in the sort of circles they were used to. "Boys," he greeted them, "let's get this over with."

A pint was placed in front of him without asking. Dylan eyed him with suspicion. Why call them *boys?* The sons of Eddie and Fletcher Blackburn were not to be infantilised. Were the capos planning on making a move?

"First things first. When's the next shipment due? Decker's crew's running low, and my guys are onto the dregs."

Theo inflated his chest. "Some lads arrived in from Malaga yesterday. They're at the safe house in Craster until—"

"I'm not talking that small fry shit," said Hurls, folding his arms. "There's only so much coke a group of chavs can swallow or stick up their arses. We need kilograms, not milligrams."

"Friday," Dylan answered. "Six kilos coming into NCL from Tenerife by way of Sierra Leone."

That got his attention. Had he thought Dylan had been sat around on his arse since Monday? No, it was business as usual.

"You've got it coming direct?"

"Why give the Scousers a cut when we can bring in our own?"

Hurls pursed his lips. "Who you using?"

"AJ and Maggie." Andrew James Peters and Margaret Peters were two of their best mules. No one suspected a couple in their sixties who looked like university professors. Maggie was a genius when it came to smuggling coke in her luggage. Not only did she do things like hide smaller baggies inside sanitary towels and empty shampoo bottles, but she would surreptitiously drip sardine oil onto the suitcases of other passengers on their flight. The sniffer dogs couldn't resist.

Hurls nodded his approval. "And the cleaners?"

"Fully vetted." AJ and Maggie would collect their luggage from baggage claim and visit the toilets before immigration. There, they would strike up a conversation with the hard-working cleaners and drop their supplies into the cleaning trolleys when no one was looking. The cleaners would remove the drugs from their trolleys before finishing their shift. AJ and Maggie would walk through immigration clean as whistles.

If Dylan didn't know better, he'd say Hurls was disappointed. He'd wanted him to fail.

"Anything else," Dylan asked, getting to his feet. He had collections to tend to.

"Yes, actually." Hurls folded his arms and his minder mimicked him. *Monkey see, monkey do.* "I have a problem, which means Morrison has a problem."

Morrison worked directly for Fletcher; he was on the second top rung of the ladder.

"One of the boys we have working over in Arthur's Hill hasn't been handing over all that we're owed. I know he's had clients round the clock—we've been watching the house—but he's only forking over two-thirds of what it should be. Been going on for months."

"What do you want me to do about it?"

Anger flickered in Hurls's eyes. "I want you to scare the shit out of him, that's what. We're owed a couple of grand. Find out where it is. Morrison will meet you on Thursday. He's busy until then."

Dylan ground his teeth. "Theo can do it."

Theo's mouth flopped open. "Careful, cuz. Morrison asked Hurls to ask *you*. Besides, I'm busy Thursday." He said it flippantly and with a wave of his arm as if the idea of shaking down a rent boy was beneath him.

Dylan hated taking orders from Hurls, but he hated taking orders from Theo more. He knew what his cousin wanted. One poxy business course at the college—which he failed—did not mean he could run this family.

COOPER PLACED A CHOCOLATE muffin and a cup of lukewarm tea in front of Charlene Blackburn.

"Thank you," she said, tucking straight into the muffin.

Charlene was a mess after a night in custody, but the news that she was no longer a suspect due to her short stature had brightened her complexion.

Despite her relief, Charlene's face was still marked with grief, and she hadn't stopped crying since they'd brought her in.

"Tell me more about Fletcher's boys," Cooper asked. "I met them yesterday, they're both tall, just like their dad."

"All the Blackburn men are tall. Lily must take after her mother."

"Should we start with George?"

Charlene hugged the cup of coffee in both hands. "Well, George isn't like the other Blackburns. If he didn't have Fletcher's height and eyes, I'd say he was adopted."

"What do you mean?"

"He's nice," she said with a half-smile. "I mean, Fletcher was nice, when he wanted to be, but firmness and hostility came naturally to him. George is meek and quiet; he doesn't have a violent bone in his body. Even Hazel had a vicious streak. I never met her, but I heard she'd raise her hands to the children."

Cooper couldn't help but show her repulsion in her expression. She couldn't imagine raising a hand to her daughter. Cooper's parents had smacked her from time to time under the guise of discipline. It was normal in those days she supposed. *In those days?* It was only the nineties. Still, to Cooper, smacking was nothing more than lazy parenting and an abuse of trust.

"George isn't like them," Charlene continued. "He's not cut out to do what Dylan does. He's not built for it. I mean, he's tall, but he's scrawny. He couldn't intimidate anyone. He's too sensitive."

"What did Fletcher think of that?"

Charlene sighed. "He would tease him. He'd call him..." Her voice faded away. "He'd call him names that we're not supposed to use anymore. Fletcher was from a different generation. He didn't go in for any PC stuff."

"I know a few people he would have got on with," Cooper said, thinking of Superintendent Howard Nixon.

"George is a bright boy. He's a bookworm and always has been. He's good with numbers too. That's why Fletcher had him do the accounts."

Cooper nodded. "What about Dylan?"

She flinched.

"You know," Cooper continued, "you cower every time I say that name. Are you scared of Dylan?"

She played with a silver bangle on her left wrist.

"Charlene?"

"Everyone's scared of Dylan. You've seen him." Her voice was shaky. "Can't believe I used to feel sorry for him."

"Why?"

Charlene rubbed her mouth with her hand. "Do you know why his head is shaped like that?"

Cooper shook her head.

"Because of Fletcher." She looked ashamed just for saying it. "He kicked Dylan... When he was still in Hazel's womb. When he was born, his skull was misshapen.

Cooper had to work hard not to grab Charlene and ask her why in God's name she could fall for a man who'd kicked his pregnant wife in the stomach. She found herself agreeing with Dylan's appraisal of Charlene. The only explanation was money.

"I didn't know," Charlene said, by way of an explanation. "I didn't know that story when I married Fletcher. I don't know if he mellowed with age or if he and Hazel were simply a toxic match, but he never put his hands on me. Not once. The Fletcher I knew was a gentleman."

"How did you meet?"

"I was a dancer. At Stilettos."

In other words, she was a stripper. "Ah," said Cooper, recognising the name of the bar from the list Dylan had given her.

"Fletcher would come in once a week."

"To collect protection money?"

She shrugged. "I guess so. I didn't know that at the time. This was before Eddie went to jail and I just thought of Fletcher as a regular. He could easily have someone else do it, but he had an eye for the ladies. I think he liked coming to the clubs. He'd come in every week and we'd chat. He'd always buy me a drink, but he never asked for a lap dance or say anything lewd. We'd just chat for ages. I told him I was a fan of Hemingway, and the next week he came in with a first edition of *The Old Man and the Sea* for me. It was a few months before he asked me out. After that, I never worked there again."

Cooper gave her a supportive smile. That was quite the fairytale.

"I know people think I'm a gold digger, but I was earning good money dancing for rich idiots—really good money. I had a lot saved up. Dylan has me all wrong."

"And you're too scared of him to set him straight?"

Charlene gave a nervous laugh. "George told me he was sent to a special school because everyone assumed he was slow... because of his head. Dylan would fall asleep at his desk because he couldn't sleep at home due to Hazel and Fletcher's arguing.

The nuns who ran the school didn't take kindly to him sleeping in class so they'd beat him. Then, because of how he looked, he was a target for bullies and would get beaten up by the other kids at lunchtime."

"It doesn't sound like he had an easy life."

"You don't know the half of it. The nuns would tell Hazel he'd been naughty at school and then Hazel would give him the belt. All he ever knew was violence. Then one day, his growth spurt kicked in, and he realised he was big enough to fight back. So he did. He never took crap from anyone again once he knew his fists could protect him. Fletcher, Hazel, those bloody hypocrite nuns... They created a monster."

- Chapter 14 -

While Cooper chatted to Charlene Blackburn and tried to find out any more details that might help the case, Tennessee travelled into Newcastle to talk to the owners of the eight bars who Fletcher Blackburn had been due to visit on the day he died. The young DS parked near Central Station and jogged across two lanes of heavy traffic to nip into a branch of Greggs. He bought a chicken bake, a sausage roll and a beef and vegetable pasty. His haul would hopefully keep him going until lunch. *If* he got lunch. It wasn't guaranteed these days, and devastatingly, any food waiting for him when he returned home was bound to be vegan.

Finding a bench, Tennessee tucked into his sustenance and fought off a couple of aggressive pigeons. A techie with an eye for detail had done him a solid favour and identified the hotel where Hazel Blackburn was supposedly staying. According to Tripadvisor, there were almost two thousand hotels in Barcelona, and because Hazel hadn't tagged the hotel in any of her posts, they'd had to use some detective work to narrow it down. The hotel had a rooftop bar; that narrowed it down to a more manageable one hundred and thirty-one. In the background of some of Hazel's photographs, four spires from the *Sagrada Familia* could be seen rising into a perfectly blue Spanish sky. Gaudi's unfinished basilica couldn't have been far away. They estimated it was within a mile and that brought the list down to only five hotels. They could have stopped there and simply looked through the photographs of each hotel until they found the one they wanted, but the techie had noticed that the basilica was to the south of the hotel, and that brought their list down to one: *Hotel de Tranquilidad*.

Tennessee made the call and prayed that whoever was staffing the desk spoke English. To his surprise he was greeted by Zara, a Geordie lass having a gap year in Catalonia.

"And you're sure? Ms Blackburn is definitely staying there?" he asked.

"Definitely. I saw her at breakfast. I can try her room, but I'm ninety-nine per cent sure I saw her get on the tour bus to Montserrat this morning."

"No, that's okay, Zara. Could you tell me if you saw Ms Blackburn on Monday the seventeenth of June?"

There was one direct flight from Barcelona to Newcastle per day, but it was also possible to go via Paris or Amsterdam. Technically, Hazel could nip into Newcastle, kill her ex-husband and be back in Barcelona in time for happy hour.

"Oh, goodness. Erm... I can tell you I've seen her most mornings. She likes to get to breakfast early so she can get one of the seats in the sunshine, but I don't know if I've seen her every single morning."

Tennessee thought for a moment about what Ronnie Rogers had told them earlier. "Would you say Ms Blackburn a tall lady?"

"No. She's smaller than me, and I'm five-one. Should I ask her to call you when she gets back?"

He told her not to bother. Hazel had a decent alibi and was even shorter than Charlene was. With his mind at ease, he shooed yet another bloody pigeon away and returned his focus to whatever Fletcher had been up to on the morning of the day he died.

Bambi Bar was tucked away down a side street called Pink Lane. The bar was situated on the upper floor above a nail bar and Thai massage parlour. If you didn't know it was there, you'd never spot the entrance. A small sign on an unremarkable door showed a picture of a young deer next to a flourished letter B. Tennessee checked he didn't have any crumbs on his shirt then pressed a buzzer and stared into a camera.

"Members only," came the reply.

The DS held up his ID. There was a pause and a stifled swear word before the door clicked open. A man in a cheap suit, with thinning hair and bird shit on his left shoe, met Tennessee at the top of the stairs.

"DS Daniel. Northumbria Police. Are you the manager?"

"Frank. Frank Ashman. And, yeah, you could say that."

Tennessee could smell stale cigarette smoke coming from fabric-covered chairs and barstools. A couple of ashtrays backed up his theory that Bambi Bar didn't observe the smoking ban. The venue was one long main room with doorways branching off to other rooms. A metallic bar was in the centre, staffed by suspiciously young women in cropped tops and booty shorts. A lone customer sat huddled over a pint glass with a tatty newspaper. He adjusted his posture so Tennessee couldn't see his face.

"I'd like to ask you some questions about Monday."

Frank's shoulders stiffened. "I don't care what you've heard. None of our barmaids are on the game."

Tennessee thought Frank doth protest too much. He suspected that behind the closed doors to the other rooms, he would find beds, and God knows what else.

"I'm sure they're not," he said dryly. "Now cut the bull. I'm here about Fletcher Blackburn."

Frank looked suddenly nervous.

"When did you last see him?"

Frank rubbed his neck. "Not in a long time. Years."

"He wasn't here on Monday?"

"No. His son is a regular though."

Tennessee sighed. "I said cut the bull. Dylan's not a regular. He comes here to collect protection money, right?"

"Erm..." A bead of sweat formed in the centre of Frank's forehead.

"Relax, Frank. It's not like I'm going to tell him you snitched. Dylan gave me the list of bars he was going to visit on Monday voluntarily. He was due to come by, wasn't he?"

A single nod.

"But he didn't?"

Another nod of agreement.

"And Fletcher came instead?"

"No. I told you. I ain't seen him in years."

"What about his bodyguard?" Tennessee pulled up a picture of Ibrahim on his phone.

Frank studied it then shook his head. "No. Ain't seen him either."

"Did anyone representing the Blackburns come in that day?"

Frank led Tennessee away from the bar and his only customer. "No. Dylan was in the month before. As usual. He's like clockwork. But business has been slow lately, which meant I was light by fifty quid. I was expecting a bit of a kicking, was beyond relieved when he didn't show."

Tennessee noted it all down. "So, to be clear, you haven't seen any Blackburns in over a month?"

"Swear to God."

"And you were here on Monday?"

"Yeah. From about ten in the morning to..." He thought about it. "To probably just after midnight."

"Can anyone corroborate that?"

Frank looked even more worried than he had a moment ago. "The barmaids. Gilly and Lola were working Monday. They're not in again until Friday. I can give you their numbers?"

Tennessee waited while Frank scribbled down two phone numbers. Bambi Bar was truly a depressing place. No wonder business was slow. It needed a deep clean and a visit from vice. As he descended the stairs, ready to walk the short distance to McDermott's, Tennessee couldn't help but contemplate what he'd heard. Fletcher hadn't been to Bambi Bar to collect his money. Had he gone to any of the other venues? And if not, where the bloody hell had he been?

JUST OVER A MILE away, Paula Keaton was reversing into a rare parking space at the Royal Victoria Infirmary. She locked the car and approached the Great North Children's Hospital.

"Good morning. DS Paula Keaton." She flashed her ID at the woman sat at the desk. "I called yesterday. I need to speak to..." She pulled a notepad from her pocket and double-checked the name. "Danielle Cutmore."

The woman's eyes moved back and forth between Keaton's face and the image of her on her ID card. Satisfied, she put down her pen and asked Keaton to take a seat. "She's assisting a patient right now. I'll let her know you're here."

Keaton's boot tapped loudly against pale flooring as she waited. She wasn't impatient, she just hated hospitals, and the name *Cutmore* made her uneasy. Who would want a nurse or a doctor with that surname?

"Detective?"

Keaton jumped to her feet and shook hands with a diminutive woman with white curls and a broad face. "I'm Sister Cutmore. I was told you wished to speak with me about Millie Hanson." She led the way down a corridor to what looked like a break room. "I hope you understand that I can not give out any information that would jeopardise patient confidentiality."

"Actually, it's not Millie I need to ask you about: it's her father."

The ward sister's brows lowered. "I don't follow, dear."

Keaton glanced out the window at a group of men who were smoking in the car park. They were hooked up to IVs, and two of them needed canes to walk. Illness and immobility weren't going to come between them and their nicotine hit. "I'm investigating a serious crime that occurred on Monday. Mr Hanson is helping us with our inquiries. He told me his daughter was being treated here for measles."

"For complications related to measles, yes. We wouldn't treat her in this ward if she was still contagious. There are too many sick children with weakened immune systems. Any outbreak would be devastating."

Keaton didn't know if Hanson's daughter hadn't been vaccinated on medical grounds or if her parents believed the conspiracy theories surrounding childhood vaccinations, but either way, she hoped Millie made a full recovery.

"Mr Hanson told me he was here all day on Monday, but I noticed while I was sitting in the waiting area that visiting hours are only two till four and six till eight. Is that right?"

"Yes, and no," she replied. "Those are the official visiting hours, but it's really at the discretion of myself or the doctors. Millie's pneumonia has been severe; naturally, her parents have been anxious to stay by her side. He arrived at about ten in the morning. I remember because two women were arguing over whether the television in the family area should be showing *Homes Under the Hammer* or the *Teletubbies*." She rolled her eyes at Keaton. "He stayed with Millie until lunchtime then he nipped out for a half-hour and came back with a stuffed toy and a meal deal. When Mrs Hanson arrived with their sons in the afternoon, he left for an hour, maybe two."

Keaton paused. Half an hour was nowhere near enough time for Hanson to drive to Morshaw Manor, kill Fletcher and Ibrahim, hide the gun and return home, but two hours was doable. Forty minutes there, forty minutes back. Probably more like thirty-five minutes; he didn't seem the sort to obey the speed limit. That left fifty minutes to fire four shots, clean up and get out. It was possible. Keaton didn't know if Hanson had done it, but she knew one thing: he was a liar. He'd told her and Martin that he'd been at the hospital all day.

"What time did he leave in the afternoon?

Sister Cutmore sighed. "I'd say half two. I can't be certain."

"And he returned between half three and half four?"

"Yes. It was before I finished my shift at five."

Keaton thanked Sister Cutmore and left under a haze of annoyance. She should have known Hanson was hiding something. She knew he was a lying piece of dirt, but now he was a lying piece of dirt with no real alibi.

IT WOULDN'T HAVE TAKEN long to get back to HQ, but Keaton somehow hit every red light on the way. The traffic gods were not her side today. When she entered the lobby, Martin was waiting expectantly.

"How'd it go at the hospital?"

"His alibi's a crock of shit," she muttered, taking the stairs to CID. "He told us he was at his daughter's bedside all day, didn't he? He didn't tell us he popped out for a few hours in the early evening."

Martin was out of breath at the top of the stairs. "Don't look at me like that."

"Do your teammates know you've got the stamina of an asthmatic sloth?"

Martin put his hands on his hips and took a deep inhalation. "I'm fit as a fiddle."

"Aye, looks it," Keaton laughed. She pushed open the double doors and claimed a table at the far end of the department.

"The thing is," Martin started, "If Hanson was guilty of killing Fletcher and Ibrahim, why would he doctor the diary to make it look like they'd had a meeting? It doesn't make sense."

Keaton frowned. "What do you mean doctored?"

"Look." Martin opened a cardboard folder and removed some photographs. Keaton recognised them as the photographs she'd shown Cooper of Fletcher Blackburn's planner. He'd owned a leather-bound journal with lined paper that had been open on his desk at the time of the shootings and was, as a result, covered in red blood spatter.

"This is Monday's entry," he said, jabbing his finger at the image.

"Yes. I know. *Monday seventeenth. Family meeting at nine-thirty. Tennis at eleven. Wayne Hanson at two."*

Martin's face spread into a smirk. "I didn't say read. I said *look*."

What was he on about? Keaton pulled the images closer and squinted. "It doesn't say two o'clock. It says fourteen hundred hours."

"Exactly."

Keaton continued to scan through some other photos, images taken from various pages in the diary, not just of the day when Fletcher was killed. "He always uses the twelve-hour clock. Ten a.m., eleven a.m., three p.m. I don't see a single other entry using the twenty-four-hour clock."

"I've been through all the photographs," Martin said. "That's the only one. Add to that, the handwriting doesn't match. Now, before you say anything about handwriting analysis being largely debunked, hear me out because there are noticeable differences."

Keaton hunched over the photographs as if she was shortsighted and needed to be within three inches of the prints to read anything. "The looped Y in Wayne?"

"Do you see any other looped Ys? Or Gs, or Js?"

Oh, he was a clever boy. Keaton grinned at Martin. "I think you're onto something. I don't think Fletcher wrote this."

He pushed a rogue strand of hair back into place. "So, who did? Who would use military time?"

"Ibrahim would. He was in the army." Keaton folded her arms. "But why would he want to frame Hanson?"

"It's not framing someone if they're really guilty. We still don't know where Hanson was when he said he was at the hospital."

"You're right," Keaton said. "There's a gaping hole in his alibi and he either killed Fletcher or someone wants it to look like he did."

"Or someone left us a clue?"

Keaton gathered up the photographs. "We need to speak to Coop."

- Chapter 15 -

Cooper removed her shoes and walked barefoot across Longsands beach towards a spot Keaton and Martin had picked out. It was a mile of golden sand and award-winning clean water. To outsiders, it was a spot of postcard-worthy beauty. To natives of the northeast, it was just one speck on the one hundred mile stretch of stunning coastline that they'd been blessed with. Best not make a song and dance about it though. The longer the rest of the country thought it was *grim up north*, the longer the locals could keep it for themselves.

Martin waved a wooden fork above his head when he spotted Cooper's approach. A few steps further and she could smell the vinegar of their fish and chip lunch.

"Get 'em while they're hot," Martin said with a mouthful of fish.

The sun was high in the sky, beating down on the top of Cooper's head. She pulled a baseball cap from her bag to protect her scalp while Keaton dished up one more portion of grub.

"Don't say a word," Cooper said as they collectively looked at the odd combination that was a cap with a smart suit. "The last thing I need is a sunburned head."

The four detectives weren't the only ones taking a moment to appreciate the baking hot June day. In the northeast, whilst you were always guaranteed a winter, you weren't always guaranteed a summer. It made sense to get outdoors and enjoy the vitamin D while you could. Mums with children too young to go to school were building sandcastles. Teenagers queued up outside Crusoe's café to grab a bite on their lunch breaks and hold hands as they strolled through the shallows. Dog walkers were confined to the north end of the beach, and a lone windsurfer was optimistically trying to right his sail despite the lack of wind.

"The water looks nice," Keaton said as she handed Cooper a cardboard tray of cod and chips with extra batter. "You looking forward to swimming in the triathlon?" There was a soupçon of sarcasm to her voice that indicated she knew fine well what Cooper's answer would be.

"About as much as I'd look forward to dancing naked on the Tyne Bridge." Cooper's heart suddenly darkened. What was supposed to be a silly quip dredged up memories from the spring. She didn't know if anyone from her team had seen the footage captured on the hidden camera Kenny Roberts had placed in her bedroom, but the embarrassment still stung. She hadn't done anything wrong, apart from being naive and trusting, but still, she felt like a prize fool. At least no one in the team seemed to notice her shift in mood. The conversation about the upcoming triathlon continued without her input until Tennessee arrived and nudged her shoulder.

"Isn't that Tina?"

A group of girls in school uniforms walked arm-in-arm, their giggles carrying far and wide. Tina was on the end of the row, and her free arm dragged her school bag through the sand, leaving a trail that looked like a giant snake had slithered through it. Tina usually spent every free moment she had with Josh, and their usual lunchtime hangout was the library. Josh was nowhere to be seen, and whilst Cooper was happy for Tina to widen her social group, she was worried she was missing something. Had they had a fight? She also wondered about the girls. Tina stayed clear of popular girls; she'd been burnt before by fake friendships, rumour mills and bitchiness. Cooper considered waving, but she didn't want to embarrass her daughter, especially if she was making new friends and even more so because she was wearing a baseball cap with a smart suit. These looked like trendy girls with overly straightened hair, HD brows and skirts rolled over at the waistband. Just as she was about to turn back to her lunch, Tina spotted her. She didn't look horrified, in fact, she beamed at Cooper, ran over, said *hi* to everyone, stole a handful of chips and scampered off again.

"Who are they?" asked the girl in the middle of the chain.

"That's my mum and her team," Tina answered.

"The detective?" one asked. She appraised the team as they sat in the sand.

"Yeah." Tina pulled in her lips as she often did when she was nervous.

"Hey, Ms Cooper!" another girl called out. "Thanks for locking up Mr Hutchins. I heard you lifted him above your head like a wrestler and slammed him on the school car park so hard his head exploded."

Cooper let out a laugh. "Actually, I slipped on the ice, and it was *my* head that was bleeding. DS Keaton here was the one who tackled him to the ground."

The girls made a collective, "Cool." Without an invitation, they sat down and bombarded the team with questions about the Tarot Card Killer.

After ten minutes, Tina checked her watch. "We have to go. Biology starts in five."

While the girls picked up their things, Cooper mouthed to Tina, "Everything okay?"

Tina shrugged. "I'll see you at home. Will you be back for dinner?"

Cooper wondered what that answer meant. "I'll be back by six. I promise."

With the teenagers trudging back up the beach with less pep in their steps than had been there earlier, talk returned to their current caseload.

"Why would Ibrahim put a fake entry in the diary?" asked Tennessee. "Did he want Fletcher to think he was meeting Hanson?"

"I don't think he did. I think someone just wanted it to look like Ibrahim wrote it," Martin said.

Cooper wrinkled her nose, and for a second, she resembled a bunny rabbit. “Perhaps it’s neither. The killer might have written that entry in to throw our attention on to Hanson but didn’t take the time, or have enough time, to mimic Fletcher’s handwriting that closely.”

Keaton picked up a handful of sand and let it filter through her fingers. “You don’t think Ibrahim was working for the Roker Boys on the side, do you? Perhaps he put the entry in the diary on their orders but ended up getting killed himself.”

“To leave no witnesses?” Martin added.

“That’s really the only explanation we’d have for the Roker Boys gaining access to Morshaw,” Cooper replied. “Even without the armed guard, the place was well protected. High walls, electronic gates, dogs, cameras...”

Keaton continued to play with the sand. “We should collect handwriting samples from the family.”

Cooper nodded. “I want authentic samples. Things they’ve written at home when they’ve been relaxed, without a detective looking over their shoulders. When the SOCOs are finished with the house, we’ll have a mooch around and look for notepads, shopping lists, diaries. Anything like that.”

Everyone agreed.

“Tennessee, what did you get from the bars? And you said you wanted to rule Hazel Blackburn out?”

Tennessee finished a mouthful of fish and cleared his throat.

"Yeah. She's still in Spain. The receptionist recalls seeing her each morning for breakfast. Now it's possible to fly to Newcastle, murder two people and fly back to Spain in the course of a day, but it's a long shot. Also, she's shorter than Charlene, and I don't see how she'd get past the guard after what Lily told us."

"Fair enough," Cooper said. "What about the bars?"

"I don't know who the owners are more frightened of, us, or the Blackburns. Probably the Blackburns to be honest. I spent most of the morning trying to get them to admit that they were being extorted let alone tell me when they last saw Fletcher or Dylan." He pulled his notepad from his pocket and flicked the pages around a spiral wire until he found the information he was after. "Fletcher got to Feisty's first. The owner, Misha Rudd, told me he got there at quarter past twelve on Monday. He didn't hang around and was out the door as soon as he had his cash."

Cooper nodded. She knew Feisty's and its owner from a troubling case she'd worked earlier in the year. A case that saw her having to arrest her own colleague.

"Approximately ten minutes later, he was at the Silver Mirror. It's a pole dancing club. Fletcher bought one of the girls a drink and stayed for a while. The girl's called Sarah Lewis but goes by Sasha. She says he was a gentleman and left her a fifty quid tip. Doesn't recall seeing anyone going by Ibrahim's description. He may have waited in the car, might have been watching the exits. Who knows. It was twenty past one when he got to LOL. It's a nineties theme bar. The manager said Fletcher was looking a bit peaky but otherwise didn't have anything to report."

"What did she mean by peaky?" Cooper asked. "Nervous? Ill?"

"I asked, but she couldn't really say. Said she'd met him a handful of times and he'd always come across as a strong, larger than life character, but on Monday he didn't seem himself. It was about twenty to two when he got to Vixen. Vixen calls itself a gentlemen's club, but it's just another strip joint. Aleksei Pavlovich, the owner, said he introduced Fletcher to a redhead named Darcy Houston. He and Darcy flirted for a while but then his mood shifted and he wanted to leave. He got his money and left."

Cooper raised a brow. "She turned him down?"

"Perhaps. I haven't spoken to her yet. After that... I'm at a loss because Fletcher didn't make it to McDermott's or Bambi Bar."

"I wonder why?" Cooper pondered out loud while Keaton and Martin scrunched up the rubbish from their fish and chips into a ball. "Something made him go home. Did he get a call to lure him back to Morshaw?"

"I'll get onto the phone companies," Keaton offered.

"Thanks, Paula. And while you're at it, find out where Hanson actually was. You and Martin go and have a chat with him. Tell him we know there's a gap in his alibi that coincides with the time Fletcher's movements became unaccounted for. He can either tell us what the bloody hell he was up to, or we can arrest him for murder—his choice. Tennessee, we'll head back to Budle Bay and speak with George Blackburn. He's the only immediate family we haven't really spoken to yet."

Tennessee nodded. "And Theo. We should speak to him."

Cooper agreed. "And won't that be something to look forward to?"

"Like a hole in the head."

- CHAPTER 16 -

TENNESSEE USED THE DRIVE to Budle Bay as an opportunity to call his wife, Hayley, and check in on her and little baby Alfie. Cooper couldn't hear Hayley's half of the conversation, but she picked up a happier tone to her voice than she'd heard of late. It was a good sign. Hayley put Alfie on the phone to speak, or gurgle, to his Dad and Tennessee sang a number of nursery rhymes to his son while he and Cooper zipped through the Northumbrian countryside. When they arrived at the Blackburns' barn conversation, they found Lily in the garden reading a copy of Marie Claire. She cut a stylish figure in a pair of bug-eyed shades, skinny jeans and a floaty, bat-wing jumper. Inspired by Tennessee's concern for his loved ones, Cooper sent a quick text to her mother. *How's Dad?*

Lily lowered her shades for the briefest of seconds and asked, "Where's Charlene? Why are you still holding her?"

Cooper and Tennessee shared a look. "Actually," Cooper said, making sure to keep her voice neutral, "New evidence came to light and Charlene is no longer considered a suspect. She was released this morning."

Lily looked put out. She pulled her phone from a designer handbag and marched towards the house. "Charlene? The police said you'd been released... You have! About time too. Where are you? Do you need a lift?"

The door to the barn closed and Cooper and Tennessee were left in the courtyard twiddling their thumbs until George emerged with a tray of drinks.

"Sparkling water?" he asked. The ice cubes chimed against the glasses as he walked. He placed the tray on the patio table and took a seat. "I assume it's my turn to *have a little chat*. I overheard Lily. Is it true? Is Charlene free to come home?"

Cooper nodded; he seemed relieved.

"I never thought she was capable of something like that."

Cooper and Tennessee sat opposite George. Tennessee removed a notepad and pen and waited for Cooper to begin.

"George, I wanted to ask you about your relationship with your father."

George scoffed and ran his finger up the edge of his drink, snaking a trail through the condensation that was forming on the outside of the glass. "What relationship? It certainly wasn't one of father and son. We were employer and employee." He paused to look at the sky. "Actually, I didn't have much of a choice in the matter so it would be more accurate to say we were master and slave. I used to be jealous of other families. I knew my family was wealthy, and I was supposed to be grateful, but I was always jealous of the poorer kids at school. They'd come in on a Monday and talk about what they'd been up to with their families. Building a den in the woods with their dad. Making a pie with their mum. Putting the sofa cushions on the floor and camping out in the living room. We never did anything like that. In Morshaw, it wasn't a case of children should be seen and not heard, it was a case of children should stay the hell out the way at all times. Until we were old enough to be useful, that is."

Cooper felt terrible for him. There was clearly an unhealthy dynamic to the Blackburn clan.

"Yesterday," she started, "when I said I was sorry for your loss, you snorted. Did you doubt my sincerity, or are you glad your father is dead?"

George leant back so that the sunshine covered his face while he considered the question. He stayed like that for a good twenty seconds before adjusting his posture again. "My dad was a bad man," was all he said.

"I heard what happened to Dylan when he was younger. From what I've been told, it sounds like your father was a violent man."

"That's putting it mildly."

Cooper considered placing a hand on his arm as a comforting gesture but thought it might be overkill and reconsidered. "Tell me more," she said.

"He created a monster. You just have to look at Dylan to see that. Beat the shit out of him so he'd beat the shit out of others."

A monster. That wasn't the first time Cooper had heard that phrase used to describe Dylan.

George removed his glasses and placed them on the table. His eyes looked smaller without the glass lenses to magnify them. He pressed the heels of his palms into his eyes for a moment before continuing. "If you ask me, I'd say Dylan snapped. It's the cycle of violence, isn't it?" His voice trailed away as he gulped at his water.

Cooper noted that the young man's eyes were reddening at the edges and he didn't look like he'd had a good night's sleep in a while.

"And as for Lily," he paused to look over his shoulder, "Dad controlled every aspect of her life. The precious little princess. You know, until this happened, I'm not sure Lily even knew what Dad and Uncle Eddie did for a living. The baby girl sheltered from the big bad world. Dad didn't even like her dating. Apart from the Hanson boy. Practically whored her out to broker that deal."

"Which Hanson boy?" Tennessee asked.

"The eldest. He's called Richard. Dylan and I just called him Dick."

Tennessee's mouth twitched.

"Theo couldn't stand it. Understandably. Called Dad a dirty old pimp. Course he's the only one who could talk to Dad like that and get away with it. He basically has immunity being Eddie's son."

Cooper's forehead creased into three lines. "Why couldn't Theo stand it?"

George rolled his eyes. "Because he and Lily are a thing. It's disgusting. They're cousins. They think no one knows, but they're not that subtle, and we're not idiots." He shook his head and rolled his eyes again. This time they looked like they'd disappeared back into his skull. "So, coming back to your earlier question. Am I glad my father is dead? The answer is yes. He beat on Dylan before he was even born, he never let Lily grow up, and as for me..." He stopped himself.

"What did he do to you?" Cooper asked.

George's eyes narrowed. "I don't want to talk about it." He picked up his glass of sparkling water and threw it with all his might against the wall of the barn. The glass shattered into hundreds of tiny pieces that scattered around the courtyard. Ice cubes slid across the paving stones, and a slice of lemon came to rest by George's foot. "My dad was a bastard. The devil incarnate. He deserved to die."

Cooper had been caught off guard by George's outburst. She'd heard he was the quiet, bookish one of the Blackburn family, but perhaps that was just when he was viewed in comparison to the likes of Dylan and Fletcher.

"George," Tennessee said, his voice calm but firm, "is there anything you'd like to tell us?"

"Like if I killed my father? No. I did not. And as for Mo, I didn't want him dead. He was good to us. Excuse me for a moment. I need to wash my face." He got to his feet, picked up his glasses and walked away.

While George composed himself, Cooper put a call into Whyte, and Tennessee stroked the belly of a tortoiseshell cat that had wandered into the courtyard.

"What's the latest on Hanson?"

"Bugger all, Erica—"

"Ma'am," she corrected him.

There was a pause. "I was under the impression you hated being called ma'am."

"You're new to my team. Until we have the level of familiarity and trust that I have with the others, we'll be using the formal means of address." What Cooper didn't add was that she didn't think he'd ever reach that stage. He'd shown his true colours when they'd joined the force. "If you don't like ma'am, chief is also fine. Now, what do you mean by bugger all?"

"We've been watching him since ten or ten-fifteen. He left his home to walk to the local shop, bought a paper and some Rizlas. Didn't leave home again until noon, when he, his wife and son headed to the RVI, which is where we are now, ma'am."

There was a tension in his voice when he added *ma'am*.

"Okay. Keaton and Martin want to speak to Hanson again. Call Keaton and let her know where she can find him. Don't talk to them when they arrive. I don't want Hanson making you or Boyd. Let me know if he meets any associates."

Cooper hung up and Tennessee eyed her. "What's the deal with you and—" He cut himself off when George returned. She wondered if he thought Whyte was a former lover and things had ended badly. She trusted Tennessee and would explain her coldness to Whyte, but for now, they had more questions for George Blackburn.

"George, are you okay to continue?"

He nodded and sat down. "Sorry about that. I'm usually more controlled."

"It's a difficult time for all of you," Cooper said softly. "I'd like to take you back to Sunday when your father met with Wayne Hanson. Were you there for the meeting?"

"Yes. It was me, Dylan and Dad. Theo was there and Mo too. Hanson brought a heavy with him, but it was all very amicable. Dad and Hanson were working toward the same goal."

"Taking out the Roker Boys."

His body tensed. "Who told you that?"

"It doesn't matter," Cooper said. "So, you're saying the atmosphere was good? There was no tension between your father and Hanson?"

"It was fine. They'd been meeting regularly. They agreed on the plan."

Cooper wiped a hand over the back of her neck; she was going to burn if she wasn't careful. "What was the plan, George?"

He flashed a knowing smile. "No comment."

He wasn't silly. He didn't want to incriminate himself or his remaining family. As he wasn't under arrest, he had no motivation to share that information.

"Did your father arrange for Hanson to return on Monday?"

"No." He shook his head. "We arranged to meet again in a week's time."

"How did you spend Monday?"

He glanced sideways, recalling the day his father died. "Erm, let's see. In the morning I walked the dogs. I took them up to Keilder and hiked a five-mile trail. I got back to Morshaw at about noon, had a shower, chatted to Charlene. She wants to redesign the garden. She wanted my input—"

"You like Charlene?" Cooper asked. She'd picked up on Lily's *mummy's boy* comment.

"What do you mean *like?"*

He was sensitive to it. When no teasing remark followed, he continued.

"She's the only person in my family who never made fun of me for liking books and stuff."

"What did you do in the afternoon?"

His cheeks reddened. "I had a date."

"Who with? Where did you go?"

"Her name's Rose Watson. We met at about two next to Grey's Monument, ate at Wagamama's in Newcastle then went to the cinema in the Gate. We had a few drinks afterwards."

To her left, Cooper saw Tennessee note down the name of the restaurant. "What did you see?" he asked.

"The new Tarantino."

"Is it any good?" Tennessee asked, lifting his eyes from the notepad.

George shrugged. "It was all right. Took a while to get going."

A rumble of car tyres on gravel caused all three pairs of eyes to turn to the driveway. A silver Mercedes rolled to a stop, and a towering man with a dark ponytail and eyes the colour of coal emerged.

Cooper immediately recognised him as Fletcher's nephew, Theo Blackburn. That saved Cooper the job of tracking him down. He'd come to them.

"Erica Cooper, long time no speak," he said as he approached. He extended an arm and shook Cooper's hand. He stank of beer and was most likely over the limit. "I liked you better with long hair," he said as if Cooper cared. "You know, I think Dad had a thing for you. Pretty ladies were always his weak spot. It's the only explanation for him dishing on the other families. The Blackburns aren't rats. I bet he thinks about you while he's tucked up in bed in that cell of his. If you know what I mean."

Cooper knew exactly what he meant. It was nonsense. Eddie Blackburn did not have a thing for her, nor did she consider herself the sort of pretty lady a Blackburn boss would go for. Theo had only said it to unsettle her. It wouldn't work.

He turned to George. "Your sister at home?"

George glared at him, blinked, then tilted his head towards the barn.

As Theo walked away, Cooper placed a photograph on the table. "Do you recognise this gun?"

George swallowed. "Is this what..."

"Yes, that's the gun that was used to shoot your father and Ibrahim Moradi."

"Em..." He looked back at the house and rubbed his forehead.

"What is it?" Cooper asked.

"It's nothing. No. No, I don't recognise it."

"You do, George. I can see it in your eyes. There's no point lying to me."

He glanced at the house again and shook his head in resignation. "That's Dad's gun," he said. "He kept it hidden in his office."

Finally, they were getting somewhere. They knew who the murder weapon belonged to. Now to work out who'd used it.

Tennessee leant forwards. "Who else knew about the gun?"

George turned his head back to look at Tennessee. "Hardly anyone. Dylan, Theo, Mo and well, me. And even though we knew he had it, we never knew where to find it."

"You said he kept it in his office," Cooper reminded him.

"Yes, in his office, but beyond that, I couldn't tell you. Dad was a paranoid man. He trusted few people and to be honest, I don't think he even trusted those. I mean... look what happened. The bastard was right, wasn't he? Three times I saw that gun. Once he pulled it out of the desk drawer and stuck it in my face because I'd put a decimal point in the wrong place. Completely messed up our calculations for the new restaurant. Another time it was in a book, a fake book, one of those ones where the pages have been hollowed out."

"What had happened on that occasion?"

George turned his palms to the ceiling. "Some little chav kid from Blyth. Don't ask me his name—I have no idea—but I know he was part of Cannon's crew."

"And who's Cannon?" Cooper asked.

"He erm, he works for someone who works for Dad."

"So Cannon's a soldier?"

"Call him what you like." George was momentarily distracted by the tortoiseshell cat as it jumped on to his lap and purred loudly. He shoved it off his knee and wiped his hands on his trousers. "Allergies," he explained. "Yeah, this chav kid was selling... let's say, sweets."

"Sweets?" Cooper asked, making air quotes.

"Yeah, sweets. Anyway, he lost a bag of these *sweets*, said they'd been stolen, but Canon thought he'd kept them for himself. He owed Canon, which meant he owed Peters, which meant he owed Dad. He didn't shoot him. Just scared the crap out of him. I don't think the gun's ever been used, not until..."

"When was this?" Cooper asked, wondering if the unnamed chav kid could have been feeling vengeful.

George stared into space for a moment and exhaled. "Got to be at least three, four years ago."

Cooper concluded that unless the kid wanted his revenge served ice cold, he probably wasn't involved. "And the third time you saw the gun?"

"I saw it hidden behind the bin. I think he thought if he kept moving it, no one would be able to grab it before he could."

He'd been wrong. Someone had managed it.

Cooper got to her feet; she had all the information she needed for now. "Thank you for your time, George. I'd like to speak with Theo. Where would I most likely find him."

George rubbed his brow. "He's either raiding the liquor cabinet or doing something unspeakable to my sister."

Cooper hoped it was the former.

- Chapter 17 -

Theo Blackburn was what Cooper would describe as a workie-ticket. Nixon would say he was a good-for-nowt-piss-taker with an ego the size of St. James' Park. When Cooper asked Theo for a word, he picked up a copy of the Evening Chronicle and said. "Give me five minutes, sweetheart. I need to take a dump."

Charmed, Cooper waited outside the downstairs loo for five minutes, then she waited five more. When Theo still hadn't returned after forty minutes, she banged several times on the bathroom door.

"Can't a man shit in peace?" His voice was low and gravelly, but it cracked a few times. He wasn't angry. He was stifling a laugh and wasting her time.

Tennessee looked like he was ready to kick the door down, which gave Cooper an idea.

"Theo. You've been in there a long time. I'm becoming concerned for your safety, and as a member of law enforcement, I can legally enter a room to conduct a welfare check. If you don't want us to see you with your pants around your ankles, I suggest—"

The toilet flushed and the door opened.

"See," he said, zipping up his fly. "Alive and well."

Cooper hid her face in the crook of her elbow. "But we won't be if we stand here much longer," she muttered.

"That'll be last night's chilli."

"You don't say." Cooper's eyes were beginning to water. "Now, Theo. I need to discuss—"

"Shower first. Discussions later." He pushed past Cooper and headed for the stairs.

"Theo?" He was trying her patience.

"Come on, you know you have to have a shower after taking a shit."

Tennessee shot his arm out and blocked the stairwell. "Nice try. Now go back to the kitchen, sit down and answer our questions or—"

"Or what exactly?" Theo's expression turned from class clown to evil clown. Cooper had seen it time and time again with these alpha males. Tennessee had the height, clear skin and cheekbones of a runway model and men like Theo Blackburn didn't take kindly to being challenged by pretty boys. To be fair, they didn't take kindly to being challenged by anyone, but attractive men really seemed to get them riled up. Cooper knew exactly how to bring him back into line. She pulled out her phone and started dialling.

"What you doin'? Askin' for back up?"

Cooper smiled. "Nope." She pressed *speaker-phone.*

"Westgate Unit. HMP Frankland."

Theo's expression changed again. This time from evil clown to little boy.

"This is DCI Cooper, Northumbria CID." She recited her badge number. "I'd like a word with Eddie, please."

Theo shook his head. "All right, all right. Hang up. You made your point."

As Theo skulked off to the kitchen, Cooper winked at Tennessee. He winked back.

"Let's start with an easy one. Where did you go after the family meeting on Monday morning?"

Theo already had a can of Coors in his hand. It whooshed as he pulled the tab and he gulped down the foam before it overflowed.

"Out and about. Here and there."

"Dylan called you that morning. He said you weren't picking up."

"I was driving. You're not supposed to use your phone and drive at the same time. It's illegal. Isn't it, detective?"

Dick, Cooper thought. "Where were you driving, Theo? Start talking or I hit redial."

"All right, don't get your panties in a twist. I drove home, parked up and I went into Newcastle for a few hours then got the Metro to Sunderland. If you're looking for an alibi, I'm bound to be on camera getting the train from Haymarket to Pallgate."

"Why in God's name..." Cooper stopped herself from asking why in God's name he'd want to go to a place like that. Some of her school friends had taken places at Sunderland University and had been housed in student accommodation in Pallgate. She'd visited once or twice when her gran had offered to look after Tina, and whilst she was sure the place had improved in the last fifteen or so years, she had no desire to go back based on what she'd seen at the time. She rephrased it. "Why were you in Newcastle, and why did you go to Sunderland?"

He drank, then he drank some more. "I fancied a few drinks."

"On a Monday?" Tennessee asked.

"It's as good a day as any."

Tennessee shrugged at Cooper. He couldn't argue with that. "So, these bars and pubs you visited in Newcastle, they wouldn't have been part of your collection racket?"

"I wouldn't know anything about a collection racket."

"Course you wouldn't," Tennessee said with a wry smile. "What about in Sunderland? We know you don't control that area."

"Went to see a friend. Walked towards the centre and had a pint in Fitzgeralds before heading back."

"Isn't that a good half-hour walk?" Tennessee asked before Cooper asked the more pertinent question.

"Which friend?"

Theo put his can on the kitchen bench. "More like twenty minutes when your legs are as long as mine, and as for the other question... No comment."

"Did you meet the Roker Boys?" Cooper asked.

"Who?"

He was playing innocent.

"Come off it, Theo. We know you know who they are. Okay, humour me for a second. Your uncle and Wayne Hanson were going after their turf and you were pissed off because you weren't going to get a slice of the pie, or the slice you were getting wasn't big enough for you?"

"That's a nice theory, DCI Cooper, but my response is still *no comment*." He looked at his can of Coors but didn't take another drink. Perhaps he thought it was best to stay sober, or relatively sober. "If you want more from me, I'll be needing my lawyer."

Cooper nodded. Fair enough. She could talk to him at the station if needed. For now, she'd wait and see what alibi Wayne Hanson came up with.

"We'll be off now," she said. "Take care, Theo. Give your father my best when you speak to him. Oh, and Lily's a lucky girl."

He met her gaze. "What?"

"Lily. She's obviously in bits about losing her dad, and not having a mother around, that's tough... I bet she's grateful to have you and her brothers to turn to."

ONCE BACK IN COOPER'S shiny new car, Tennessee turned the radio on to mask their conversation while they pulled away. "Did you see how he froze up when you asked about Lily."

"He knew we'd be watching his body language, so he stayed still. Too still. He was like a statue."

"If Theo is in love with Lily..."

"And Fletcher wanted Lily to stay away from Theo and date the Hanson boy..."

"That gives Theo a motive... And he knew there was a gun in that office." Cooper turned out of the street and lowered the radio. "Do you know how bloodlines work in families such as the Blackburns?"

Tennessee shook his head. "Not really."

"Power goes from father to son unless the son isn't of age. We're not talking the age of consent or old enough to drink or vote. In families like this, they like a little more maturity. You usually need to be at least twenty-five to be head of the family."

"So when Eddie went to jail, the family passed to Fletcher because Theo would have only been, what, twenty-one?"

"Exactly. Now, are you thinking what I'm thinking?"

Tennessee slapped his hands off his thighs in a rhythm. "I'm thinking nine out of ten murders come down to sex or money. If killing Fletcher meant Theo could take the throne and be free to be with Lily, then it looks like he has twice the motive. His alibi isn't great either."

"The Metro? A little convenient. He could have killed Fletcher and Ibrahim then purposely went somewhere he knew would have cameras."

Cooper's phone rang. She fished it from her pocket and handed it to her DS. "Answer that, will you?"

"It's Nixon... Daniel here, sir. Yes, she's driving. We're heading back to HQ... Okay. Will do, sir."

"What was that about?" Cooper asked as she turned left and joined the A1.

"We need to go straight to the Freeman. Margot wants to see us ASAP."

- Chapter 18 -

As Cooper waited for the red light to change at the junction to enter the Freeman Hospital, she could feel her chest tightening. She gripped the steering wheel so firmly that the pads of her fingers began to throb. The lights turned green, but her foot remained frozen on the brake pedal. The driver behind her beeped their horn and Cooper lurched the car forward while it was still in second gear, causing it to stall. A group of young men in fluorescent vests who were waiting at the bus stop pointed and laughed.

"Coop? You okay?" Tennessee asked.

Cooper fought with the car and got it moving again. She circled the open-air car park three times. There had to be a space. There had to be. She couldn't face the multi-storey car park. Not today. Not after what happened. Was there a fucking convention on? Why wasn't there a God-damned space in *this* car park?

"Coop?" Tennessee touched Cooper's arm and she jumped. "Listen." His voice was soft but anxious. "Why don't you get out here and I'll park? I'll meet you in the morgue."

Cooper stopped the car and ran her hands over her face, they were shaking and clammy. This had happened before when she'd come to observe an autopsy on a prominent priest who'd died under mysterious circumstances. On that occasion, she'd been alone. No one had been there to witness her panic attack. She swallowed and turned to the DS. "Thank you," she said. Her mouth was dry. "I'll see you inside."

Cooper pulled herself from the vehicle and left the door open for Tennessee as he switched seats. She could barely put one foot in front of the other, and although she was outdoors and there were no walls to close in on her, she felt claustrophobic all the same. She forced herself to take slow breaths. Her abductor was miles away, in a secure unit, and could do her no harm. Still, she felt frightened. She pulled at her shirt, loosening it around the neck. She unfastened two buttons and didn't care if it was an unprofessional look that risked showing her bra, she couldn't stand the feeling of anything on her neck.

When she reached the hospital doors, she stopped to steady herself, aware of concerned looks on the faces of people coming and going and wondered what they must think of her. She wasn't here as a patient or relative. No one had given her life-changing news. She had to get it together.

Cooper blinked back a tear and followed her usual unmarked route to the morgue.

Tennessee caught up with her at the bottom of a flight of stairs. "Hey. Erm, I can handle this if you want to stay above ground."

Cooper smiled at him. He'd always had her back. "That's twice you've tried to step in to protect my headspace during this case. If it was anyone else, I'd be giving them an ear full."

"But as it's me?"

"As it's you, I'll give you a pat on the arm and tell you I'm fine."

"You sure? You still look a little green around the gills."

"Well we're about to go into the morgue, so I'm probably going to look greener than the Tyne Bridge in a minute. You ready?"

Tennessee was notoriously weak around the dead.

"As I'll ever be."

He pushed open a set of double doors and led the way along a corridor and into an observation room. The temperature, which usually chilled Cooper to the bones, was a pleasant relief from the heatwave occurring outdoors.

From the observation room, they watched forensic pathologist Margot Swanson at work. She was elbow deep in a man who must have weighed over two hundred kilograms. She lifted out the man's heart, set it on an electronic scale, noted the weight and caught sight of her guests.

"Oh, hello there," she said. "Give me a minute to clean Mr Warner up, and I'll be right with you."

She concluded what she was doing, removed her gloves and apron and placed them in a specialist bin before removing her face mask and goggles. She approached a filing cabinet that was set in the corner of the room and fingered her way through it until she found the file she was after. "Do you want to come through?" she asked.

Cooper and Tennessee shared a look, then they shook their heads synchronously and beckoned Margot to come to them instead. Otherwise, there was a chance some poor orderly would have to clean up Tennessee's vomit, or her own, or both.

"Let's get down to business, shall we?" Margot started in her melodic Highlands accent. She opened her file and handed Cooper her report. "Ibrahim Moradi. Homicide. Cause of death was loss of brain function due to a gunshot wound to the head. Fletcher Blackburn. Homicide. Cause of death was cardiac arrest due to gunshot wounds to the chest."

Cooper and Tennessee waited. This was one of those *no shit, Sherlock* moments. You didn't need a degree in forensic pathology to work that out. Margot was teasing them. She was holding something back—but what?

"But?" Cooper pressed.

"But, I thought you'd like to know that Fletcher was already dying."

"Well, he was getting on in life," Tennessee said. "I doubt he lived a very healthy lifestyle."

"He was only fifty-two," Margot snapped, "and there was nothing wrong with his cardiovascular system."

He'd touched a nerve and Cooper tried not to smirk.

"I was curious after I spotted yellowing in Fletcher's optical media and even more so after I examined his stomach. I sent some samples to toxicology, and as suspected, he displayed high levels of digoxin."

Cooper straightened up. "And what's digoxin when it's at home?"

"It's used fairly commonly in heart medications. It's usually prescribed as digitalis and is used to treat atrial arrhythmias and congestive heart failure. Low levels of digoxin would suggest Fletcher was using one of these medications but, as I said, his cardiovascular system was in fine working order. His medical history showed no prescriptions made for such a medicine."

"But you said Fletcher displayed high levels of this digoxin."

"Exactly," Margot said, pulling her soft curls free from a hair tie and running her fingers through the locks.

"Which means?"

"Which means Fletcher Blackburn was poisoned."

- CHAPTER 19 -

DS PAULA KEATON WANTED to get back to April, open a bottle of red wine and snuggle on the sofa. They'd been together for over a year now, and April had pretty much adopted Keaton's youngest brother like he was her own child. They had become their own little family. When Keaton was all sports, crime-fighting and sullen moments, April was a bubbly, ray of light who understood her demanding role at Northumbria CID and could make the best fried chicken this side of the Atlantic. Riley, Keaton's brother, had turned up on her doorstep late last year with a black eye, a suitcase and his piggy bank. He'd stayed with them ever since.

Keaton and Martin had just left a trendy little flat in a part of Gateshead named Low Fell. "What do you think?" she asked Martin.

"I say she's telling the truth. She did give us a frightening amount of detail."

Keaton shuddered, pushed the disturbing visual away, and called Cooper. "Boss, we've just left Hanson's alibi's place."

"Back up a second," came the reply.

"Ah, sorry, boss. Martin and I visited Hanson at the RVI after Whyte called to say he was there. We took him to one side, so we wouldn't freak out his daughter, and told him we knew his alibi was bullshit and that he was not at the hospital all day like he'd told us."

"Go on."

"Well, he fessed up that he'd been with his bit on the side. A woman named Natasha Cleveland who lives in the Fell. He obviously didn't want his missus to find out."

Cooper sounded distant. She must be using speaker phone. "And the bit on the side confirmed this?"

"Yes, she backs his story."

"She would though," Cooper added. "I mean, if Wayne Hanson tells you to lie to the police, you lie to the bloody police. Unless you want your thumbs broken."

Keaton slid into the driver's seat of her car and waited for Martin to jump in the passenger side after he'd stopped to tie his laces. "We believe her. She didn't spare us the details so expect to see inches, costumes and positions in my write up."

Keaton heard a snort before she asked how Cooper was getting on.

"We've just left the morgue. Margot wanted to see us."

"You mean she wanted to see our dashing DS Daniel."

Keaton could hear Tennessee saying something in the background but couldn't make it out.

"There's been an interesting development, Paula. I'll fill you all in at the morning briefing. In the meantime, could you follow up on George and Lily's alibis? Lily said she was working at Rachel's Beauty Retreat on Pilgrim Street and George said he was on a date. He went to Wagamama's and then saw the new Tarantino at the cinema in The Gate."

"You got it, boss."

Keaton thought of April. She'd have been home for over an hour now and would have no doubt already fed the cats, picked up Riley from band practice and done some laundry. She'd be waiting for Keaton and choosing what to have for dinner. She pulled over to send a text. *Don't worry about dinner. I'll bring in Wagamama's.* Within thirty seconds, Keaton had received a string of heart-shaped emojis as the reply. She truly loved that woman.

FREEMAN HOSPITAL WASN'T TOO long of a drive from Tynemouth, perhaps fifteen minutes on a good day and with a flagrant disregard for the fifty zone on the Coast Road. Sadly, today was not a good day, and as well as hitting rush hour, there were several camera traps set up on Benton Road. Cooper had promised Tina she'd be home at six and it was ten past when she crossed the threshold.

She found Tina mopping the kitchen floor while Steven squawked at her for his next feed. His cute baby cheeps were long gone, and now he cawed as loud as his little lungs would allow.

"You're late," Tina huffed without looking up.

It was only ten minutes, but she'd have been a fool to think Tina wouldn't have noticed. "I'm sorry, T. I'm working a challenging case at the moment. I'm just pleased to have got home before midnight." She dropped her bag onto a chair at the kitchen table and watched Steven spread his wings and give them a tentative flap. "Hey, that's new. Does that mean he'll be able to fly soon?"

Tina stopped mopping to gaze upon her feathered baby. "From what I've read, I don't think he'll be ready to fledge until August."

August? That meant Cooper had to put up with at least another five weeks of Steven living in the kitchen. He had grown on her, but now he was out of his adorable, fluff ball stage, Cooper was looking forward to having her kitchen back. Not that she ever used it for more than microwaving packets of rice or reheating takeaways.

"I let him explore the back yard earlier. Thought I should get him used to the local smells. I made sure to scare next door's cat away first."

"Good idea," Cooper said, giving Tina a quick squeeze and looking in the freezer for something simple for dinner. "Pizza?"

"I made a hot pot," Tina said. "It'll be ready at seven."

Cooper appreciated Tina's efforts to help around the home. Her natural instinct was to worry that between cooking and caring for Steven that Tina's homework and grades would suffer. of course, Cooper knew there was little chance of Tina allowing that to happen. Still, there was a heaviness to Tina's voice that Cooper didn't like. Something was troubling her, and she wondered if it had anything to do with her new friends.

"What's with the new crowd?" she asked. "You and Josh haven't fallen out, have you?"

"No, Mum." Tina's tone had the aural quality of eye-rolling. "I'm just trying to widen my circle. Not put all my eggs in one Josh-shaped basket. If Josh and I did split up, I'd have no one."

"You'd have me."

"You don't count. No offence." Tina peered into the oven to check on the hotpot for a moment.

"So, who are they? Are you in the same classes?"

"The little redhead is Sarah, and the tall, skinny one is Lana. They're on the netball team. Sarah plays centre and Lana's goal attack. The other's are Lana's friends. They're all in the top sets."

"You've never hung out with your teammates much before."

Tina huffed. "That's because the team used to be made up of Shelly Smith and her friends. They all dropped out after Shelly... died."

A shiver ran down Cooper's spine. Shelly Smith hadn't simply died—she'd been suffocated.

"Anyway, we have new players now," Tina said. "I'm going to make a start on my English homework. This'll beep when it's done."

Cooper smiled. Her daughter was wise, but she wasn't entirely buying it. Tina had never liked having a lot of people in her life. She'd always had one intense friendship at a time, and until recently, that had been Josh. He was both best friend and boyfriend. She scrutinised Tina then nodded, "Okay. I'll call you when dinner beeps."

While Tina picked up her school bag and headed for her room, Cooper poured herself a cold glass of Estrella and sat down at the kitchen table. She hadn't heard back from her mother yet, but that wasn't unusual. The bar could be busy, and Julie and Ben couldn't pause the pulling of pints to reply to every text message. Still, she hoped her father was feeling better, so she sent a follow-up text. *Hey, Dad. Hope you're doing okay. Call me. E xxx.*

Her phone rang while it was still in Cooper's hand, and a quick glance at the screen told her it was Elliot Whyte. For a brief moment, she considered ignoring the call, but that wouldn't be appropriate. That was something Whyte would do. Instead, she took a deep breath and closed her eyes as she answered.

"Ma'am." To Cooper's relief, it was Saffron Boyd on the other end of the call. "Sorry. We're just across the road from the Hanson residence."

"What's the latest?"

"He's been cool as a cucumber all day. Even after Keaton showed up at the hospital to question him."

Cooper suspected there was a *but* coming.

"But..." *There it was.* "He's just blown his top."

"Why?" Cooper asked, sipping her Estrella and wondering if she was going to be called away from her beer and hotpot.

"Sorry, ma'am, no idea. We can see in his living room. The shutters are open. His phone rang a minute or so ago, and something's set him off. He's angry, like apoplectic with rage. Pacing back and forth. We couldn't hear what he was yelling from here, but he's properly pissed."

"Thanks, Saffron. I'm guessing word just got to him about the attack in Frankland last night. Can you and Whyte stick to him until nine? Let me know if he goes anywhere. I'll arrange for someone to replace you for the nightshift."

Boyd agreed and hung up. She called dispatch to have some plainclothes officers ready to replace Boyd and Whyte later that evening then checked the landline for any messages. There was just the one.

"Ms Cooper. This is Gus Laing from Redheugh Solicitors. Our client, Kenneth Roberts, has asked us to reach out to you regarding visitation rights with his daughter."

Cooper's heart felt like it had stopped. She'd had a restraining order slapped on Kenny within twenty-four hours of his arrest. He couldn't come within a hundred feet of her or make contact with her by phone, text or email. Sadly, those rules didn't extend to his lawyer. Cooper listened to the rest of the message then spotted the time it had come in: five-thirty. Tina must have heard the message. Did that explain the dourness in her voice? Perhaps. Whilst Kenny had never made Tina feel uncomfortable in his care, Tina felt betrayed by him. She'd let him into her life, bonded with him and finally formed a father-daughter relationship. Then one night this spring, Tina and Josh overheard Cooper yelling and came running down the stairs just as she was phoning the police.

The timer on the oven showed there was still at least thirty minutes until dinner was ready. Cooper took a long sip of beer to calm her nerves—Kenny had a way of making her skin crawl—and opened her laptop. She had research to be getting on with. She began with a simple Google search on digoxin. It didn't take long before she found that digoxin and digitalis were derived from foxgloves.

"All parts of the foxglove plant are poisonous," she read out loud. "Symptoms of foxglove poisoning include visual disturbances, headaches, nausea, vomiting and diarrhoea. Muscle weakness and tremors." If someone had been trying to poison Fletcher Blackburn, had they become impatient and shot him instead? Cooper hadn't spent long at Morshaw Manor and struggled to remember what plants were in the garden and surrounding flowerbeds. She swallowed her pride and called Justin Atkinson.

"Erica? Is everything okay?"

He sounded concerned. *He still cares, even after you treated him the way you did.*

"I'm okay, Justin. Sorry for disturbing you. It's actually a work thing." She listened for any sign of disappointment but could only hear the rattle of cutlery and din of chatter. He was in a restaurant.

"Oh. All right, go on."

"I spoke to Margot earlier, and she thinks Fletcher was poisoned. Digoxin."

"Foxgloves?"

"Yes." His intellect never ceased to amaze her. In the background, a female voice asked if he wanted a top-up. You didn't need to be a detective to work out that he was having dinner with Veronica Rogers. Again.

"Small doses over a long period of time lead to hallucinations. People who have ingested it report yellow halos and their vision can become tinted as if wearing yellow glasses. There's actually a hypothesis about Van Gough using digitalis, and that's why a lot of his paintings have a yellow hue to them."

"Really?"

"Yes. It's quite evident in Starry Night and The Night Café."

Cooper suspected Atkinson was enjoying the chance to discuss art. She typed The Night Café into Google and had to agree with the theory. There was an abundance of yellow in the oil painting. The felt of the billiard table was chartreuse in colour and around the ceiling lights, dabs of yellow in concentric circles implied dancing, golden halos.

"Listen," she continued. "You've spent more time at Morshaw than I have."

"And you're wondering if foxgloves grow in the garden?"

"I am."

"They do. Purple and white ones. You can see them from Fletcher's office."

Cooper nodded though Atkinson couldn't see. "Interesting."

"Very. I'll catch up with you tomorrow. I have to go. Ronnie's headed back to Manchester tomorrow morning, so the team wanted to take her out to dinner. I'm being anti-social."

The team. Cooper's mood lifted. It wasn't just the two of them, and even better, she was leaving.

- Chapter 20 -

Oliver Martin and Paula Keaton pulled up in the car park of a complex known as The Gate. The Gate housed a cinema, a casino and host of bars and restaurants. It wasn't everyone's idea of a good time, but Martin had met his first, and only, serious girlfriend there. In a German-themed pub named Wonderbar, no less. He'd always been shy around women and couldn't believe his luck when this stunner approached him and began flirting. After a stein too many he said something about her wearing a Wonderbra in the Wonderbar and immediately regretted it. Luckily, Steph saw the funny side, and after making fun of him for ten minutes, she leant in and kissed him on the cheek. He'd been on cloud nine all night after that. He and Steph had a whirlwind nine months until she took her dream job in Australia and made it clear she didn't expect him to go with her. Never mind.

Keaton and Martin arrived at the cinema just as a couple of ushers were struggling to evict a group of teenagers for throwing popcorn. Keaton flashed her badge; the teenagers suddenly remembered they were upstanding citizens, straightened their backs, closed their mouths and left without further trouble.

Keaton approached a tired-looking usher and asked to speak to a manager.

"Can I ask what this is about?"

Keaton didn't beat around the bush. "A murder."

The colour seeped from the usher's face, and she ran off in search of a supervisor. Keaton smirked.

It didn't take long for the shift manager to introduce himself and find evidence of George Blackburn having been at the cinema on Monday. He had a booking reference for the four-thirty showing under G Blackburn and the cameras caught him and a slender woman with strawberry blonde hair arriving at four-twenty.

"One down," Martin said. "How about we split up and save ourselves some time? I'll take the restaurant; you can take the beauty retreat?"

Keaton stared at him.

"What?"

Still, she said nothing.

"Fine," Martin sighed. "I'll go to the beautician's."

"Good boy. Now, remember you're there on official business. If you want HD brows or lip fillers do it on your own time."

If he didn't know that being taken the piss out of at every opportunity was part of the job and that Keaton had a heart of gold under all that muscle, he'd probably hate her. As it was, he thought she was ace.

"I'll bring you back a price list," he joked as he walked away. "I know how you like to look after your nails."

Martin didn't turn around to check, but he was sure Keaton would be flipping one nail in particular in his direction.

Rachel's Beauty Retreat was tucked away on Pilgrim Street in the heart of the city centre. Martin climbed a set of stairs and was transported from a dusty street suffering under the exhaust fumes of countless busses to an island paradise. Tropical ferns, which may or may not be plastic, filled every spare inch of floor space. Murals depicted sunny beaches and crystal water. Sounds of waterfalls and birdsong filled the room, and there was a heavenly scent of sandalwood and vanilla. A popping noise caught Martin's attention. Two young women were being served glasses of Champagne while they waited for their treatments. Behind them, Martin spotted a massage table in an empty treatment room. Tempting. Very tempting.

"Good evening, welcome to Rachel's Beauty Retreat. Do you have an appointment?"

Wow, she was beautiful. Sunkissed skin, shiny hair and lashes that were too long to be natural but not so long they looked fake. Pretty freckles, light brown hair, cupid's bow lips. She looked...just like Saffron Boyd. He knew he had a thing for the new member of the team. He'd felt it the second he'd laid eyes on her. But what would she want with someone like him? He wasn't experienced;

he'd only had one proper relationship. Nor was he in a position of power, which was her thing, apparently. He still lived with his parents, and with the rate at which he was managing to save for a deposit on his own home, he would be living with them for some time.

"Hello. No, I don't have an appointment—"

"Well we are open until nine and can squeeze in a few walk-ins. Were you after a teeth whitening treatment?"

What was wrong with his teeth? "No. I'm here about Lily Blackburn." He showed her his badge.

She gasped. "Wasn't it awful what happened? Poor Lily."

"Yes. It's very unfortunate. I was hoping you could help me with something... No, not my teeth ... I want to know if Lily was working on Monday."

"Oh, well, that's easy." She swiped left on an iPad, tapped her finger on the top left corner and seconds later a printer spat out what looked like a timetable. "This week's shifts and appointments," she explained.

She placed the sheet of paper on her desk and ran her finger down a column. "Here we are. Yes, Lily was in on Monday. She had clients from eleven until three-thirty."

"Thank you...erm?"

"Peyton."

"Thank you, Peyton. Could I have this?" Martin asked, picking up the timetable.

"Sure. Is there anything else I can help you with?"

His eyes went to the massage table again. Keaton would kill him if he kept her waiting. "No, thank you. Maybe next time."

Back out on Pilgrim Street, Martin found himself craving the birdsong and sandalwood of the spa. He arrived back at Keaton's car just as she did. She was carrying a large paper bag.

"Everything check out?" she asked, pressing a button on her key fob to unlock the car.

"She was working. What about the restaurant?"

"CCTV. They arrived at three-fifteen. He had chicken katsu; she had firecracker prawns."

A loud noise grumbled out of Martin's stomach. "You're making me hungry."

Keaton opened the paper bag and tossed a smaller bag in his direction. "Good job I got you some steamed buns."

Ace. He thought Keaton was ace.

TINA'S HOTPOT HAD DONE the trick. There was something about warm, comfort food that never failed to elevate Cooper's mood. Even in the heat of a summer's day, the best meals were the same ones Cooper craved in the dead of winter: hotpots, mince and dumplings, a vat of chilli, or a blow-your-head-off curry. Tina had remained quiet over dinner and hadn't wanted to talk about her father, though she did say something about Josh and how he thought she should at least meet with Kenny to hear what he had to say. Cooper didn't push it. She'd talk if and when she wanted to and hounding her wouldn't help things. Cooper made herself a cup of herbal tea and headed up to bed. Her brain was awash with questions, thoughts and theories and she doubted she'd be able to switch off at any time soon. And it wasn't just the case that was bothering her, it was the call from Kenny's lawyer, Atkinson and Ronnie, Tina, her father, Whyte. The list went on.

At midnight, Cooper gave up on her third attempt at counting backwards from three hundred as her way of falling asleep and instead turned to the Audible app. She downloaded an album entitled *Hello Sleep* and listened to the soothing tones of the narrator. He had her within an inch of drifting off when a memory forced its way into her consciousness.

She was stood outside of North Shields Police Station, her long hair—for it was really long back then—danced in the wind. Across the road, two children and their father played on the swings in the play area, and a man walked by with five dachshunds. She remembered it like it was yesterday. Her shift had ended. She'd taken a moment to enjoy some fresh air after an afternoon dealing with a bunch of teens who smelled like a brewery. A brewery that had been dipped in sweat and rolled in tobacco.

Whyte came jogging after her.

"Hey. Wait up, Erica."

He had fewer lines in those days. Tanned from a recent holiday and with dark brows and a down-turned nose, he reminded Cooper of a Roman soldier.

"Listen, erm... It's Friday and after a shift like that... I was going to nip to the Bell and Bucket." He looked coy. "I wondered if I could buy you a drink."

It was a chilly evening, and the idea of a cool pint in a warm, old-fashioned pub appealed to her. Not to mention that socialising with people her own age would do her some good. She lived with a baby who couldn't talk and a pensioner who did nothing but talk. But there lay the problem.

"I'd love to," she told him, "but I can't tonight—"

"Tomorrow?"

Cooper tightened her coat around her. The wind was picking up. "I can't tonight, or any night really. I have a little girl at home. My gran takes care of her while I'm at work, but I don't think it's fair if I leave her with her more than necessary."

His eyes widened. "You're a mum?"

"Yeah."

"But you're..."

"Young. I know."

He nodded. "Ah well, no harm in asking, was there? Maybe in the future?"

Cooper nodded back. "Yeah, maybe." It felt nice being asked out for a drink. Even if she couldn't take him up on the offer."

They went their separate ways, with Whyte heading back into the station and Cooper beginning her walk home. She'd got about ten paces when she realised she'd forgotten her purse. Heading back into the station, her ears pricked up when she passed the break room and heard her name.

"Whyte struck out! Shit, I had twenty quid on you. Right, who's next?"

"Jameson's next." It was Whyte's voice.

"That wet blanket? I'll give him odds of fifty to one. Doesn't stand a chance."

"None of us stand a chance." It was Whyte again. "You know she's got a bairn?"

"Nee way?"

"I'm telling ya. A baby girl apparently. Has to get home to breastfeed it or something."

"She's only nineteen."

"I know." There was a pause. "Slapper."

The break room exploded with laughter; every synonym for slapper was thrown about. Called such names because she *hadn't* gone out with him. It was illogical, stupid, insulting, infuriating...

"Tell you what, let's all go to the Bucket. I'll buy you a commiseration drink."

Cooper fled before they could see her. Tears in her eyes, she hid around the side of the building until their voices faded. Whyte had been her friend—she'd enjoyed her shifts with him—and he'd hit on her as part of some silly game of who-can-bed-the-new-girl. Cooper wiped her eyes and turned to walk home. The guys were a good thirty metres away when Whyte turned his head to glance back. He saw her crying. She could tell by his expression that he knew why, and yet he never apologised. Not once.

Cooper rolled onto her other side and stopped the track from *Hello Sleep*. It was useless. She wasn't going to sleep tonight. She might as well get her laptop and do some more research. See what she could dig up on the Roker Boys.

She crept downstairs, poured a generous shot of whiskey into a tumbler and opened her laptop. Cooper had barely typed anything into the search bar when her eyes flicked to her phone. It had been switched to silent mode, but the screen was illuminated with an incoming call.

"Dad?"

"It's me, dear."

"Mum?"

There was silence, which was usual for two reasons: Julie Cooper filled almost every moment of silence with small talk; and, at this time of night, the bar would be noisy. She should hear gregarious ex-pats singing the theme to *Only Fools and Horses*, or pint glasses being collected in, or stag groups chanting *Super Leeds, super Leeds, super Leeds United*.

"Mum? It's gone midnight. What's wrong?"

"It's your father, dear. His chest pains... I took him to the hospital, like you said, and... they got worse."

She stopped to blow her nose, and Cooper knew instinctively that something awful was coming. "Erica, he had a heart attack."

- Chapter 21 -

The first thing Cooper noticed when she entered the incident room on Thursday morning was a foil tray scattered with dark brown crumbs. Someone had brought in chocolate cake, and the gannets had demolished it before the clock had struck eight. The second thing she noticed was the huddle of men and women, some suits, some uniforms, gathered around Paula Keaton. She was sat at a table holding court.

"Silk scarves? Ooh, kinky!" Cooper heard some-one say.

Curiosity got the better of her, and she forced a gap between a young uniform and Tennessee to take a look at Keaton's notes from her interview with Natasha Cleveland. "French maid's outfit?" she asked, eyebrows peaked. "A little cliché?"

"Keep reading," Keaton urged.

Cooper scan read as childish giggles filled the room. "Oh! Wait. *He* was wearing it?"

Keaton nodded, a sly smile on her face. "It gets worse."

"I believe you." Cooper didn't need to read all the ins and outs—so to speak—she already had a pretty horrific mental image that she was trying to shake. "Okay people," she said, raising her voice to take command of the room. "Let's try our best to focus. Paula, put that file away before anyone vomits." She found her place next to the whiteboard and made eye contact with as many people as she could. "There have been a few developments. Firstly, as we've all read, Hanson has an alibi for the time of the murder." She took a red pen and drew a line through his name on the whiteboard.

"Dirty old perv," someone called out.

"Quite. Said dirty old perv was tailed all day yesterday. Saffron?"

Saffron Boyd swallowed and stood up. She wrung her hands together and spoke quietly. Was she nervous, or did she simply not like it when everyone looked at her? Cooper didn't know.

"Ma'am, em, boss. There was nothing to report until the evening when Hanson received a call and became increasingly angry. After the call in question, he paced for a while, and it was only once his wife left to take the dog for a walk, that he made a series of other phone calls, all similar in tone. He didn't leave the family home."

"Do we know who called?" Cooper asked.

"I'm waiting for the phone company to get back to me."

"Well chase them. We don't have time to waste."

"I will, boss."

Tennessee raised his hand to get Cooper's attention. "If he waited for his missus the leave, he was probably talking to the mistress. He knew we were going to speak to her, but he probably didn't count on her on giving quite so many details. Might explain his anger?"

"It could." Cooper paused, hugging a beige coloured folder to her chest. "Or, word reached him about what went down in Frankland."

"You're right," Tennessee said. "I wouldn't be surprised if he fired back in some way."

"I can guarantee he'll want revenge. We need to act quickly. Before Nixon gives himself a heart attack—" The word caught in her throat and she struggled to fight back the tears. Ben was undergoing bypass surgery to improve blood flow to his myocardium. She wouldn't be able to speak to him for hours, possibly days, so for now, she had to battle on. "Is Hanson still at home?" she directed at Boyd.

"As of twenty minutes ago. That's when I called the team who took over from us last night."

"Which brings us to the other developments." Cooper filled her lungs with air and exhaled slowly. "Regarding the murder weapon. Both Dylan and Charlene deny having ever seen the Glock. However, George tells us that not only did the gun belong to his father, but that Dylan knew about it and therefore lied to us. Now according to George, Theo would have also known that a gun was stashed in the office at all times, and Dylan told us Theo used to go clay pigeon shooting. I had someone check the SGC records; Theo Blackburn was the registered keeper of a Blaser F16 from 2016 to 2018. Prior to that, he had a Beretta DT11. His licence has expired, but young Theo was quite the marksman. He was a regional champion at fourteen and national champion at sixteen."

Around the room, people exchanged glances at the news that Theo knew how to handle guns much bigger than a Glock. 29.

"But here's the real kicker," Cooper continued. "Fletcher Blackburn may have died from gunshot wounds to his chest, but he was also poisoned."

A murmur floated through the incident room like a Mexican wave, moving from Cooper at the front to the officers right at the back. Heads turned, shoulders shrugged.

"A chemical derived from foxgloves was found in his system during the autopsy. It's highly toxic, and chances are that Fletcher was either very ill or indeed dying when he was shot."

Martin shuffled in his seat and caught Cooper's eye. "Didn't the man who owns LOL say Fletcher was looking peaky?"

Tennessee spoke in the affirmative. "Yeah. Said he was sweating and tugging on his collar."

Cooper nodded. "That makes sense."

Keaton was wiggling her pen around in the air.

"Paula?"

"Are we thinking someone got bored waiting for the poison to kick in?"

"That's what I was wondering. I've already taken the liberty of printing off the search histories from the laptops and tablets the SOCOs removed from the Blackburn residence. Printouts are in your files, but I've seen nothing to suggest any of the Blackburns were researching poisons."

"Surely they would have wiped their search history."

"I would have thought so," Cooper said. "But regardless, nothing is ever truly deleted. Tech will update us if they find anything at all relating to foxgloves or poisons. Tennessee, Keaton and Martin, we're going to Morshaw. I want handwriting samples for each member of the family. The fake entry in the diary is still a key piece of evidence. Whyte and Boyd, stick to Hanson like glue. He probably knows he's being tailed and therefore won't get up to much."

"What about the Roker Boys?" Whyte asked. "Shouldn't we put them under surveillance?"

Keaton pulled a file from within another file. "Here's what we got from Local Intelligence. No top guy as such. It's a four-way partnership. Toby Beck, Richie Boyer, Alex Deacon and Kayla Dunn."

"Kayla?" Whyte looked doubtful.

"You heard. Despite their name, the Roker Boys are shattering the glass ceiling for female mobsters everywhere."

"Go feminism," Cooper said dryly. "Nixon's not going to approve much or anything in the way of surveillance. Budgets are tight, overtime is a thing of the past, and we don't have anything to justify a warrant, let alone a phone tap. The best we can do is talk to them and get alibis for the time of the murder. Can you action it, Whyte?"

Whyte nodded. "I'll get the locals on it. Do we have the names of their capos and soldiers?"

he asked using the mafia terms for those below boss-level on the mob family tree.

"All in the file," Keaton said, handing it to Whyte. She stood up and popped on a pair of sunglasses. "Right then. It's a lovely day, let's go catch a killer."

- Chapter 22 -

Dylan Blackburn knocked on the door of a house in Arthur's Hill. The house had no door number, not that it mattered, it never received any post because officially, no one lived there. When no one answered within ten seconds, he began to knock harder and harder. A constant thunder of fist against wood until it was opened by a small, undernourished man with a haircut that made him look like a toilet brush. Dylan Blackburn was not the sort of man to wait for an invitation. He forced his way in, picked the man up in a vice-like grip and carried the starveling to the kitchen where he dropped him onto a plastic chair.

"Here, man, Dylan. There's nee need for this."

Behind him, Dylan could hear Morrison following him in and shutting the front door.

"Quiet," Dylan said. He pulled a length of rope from his back pocket and began securing the man to the chair.

"Dylan! Dylan!" His voice was filled with fear. "Whatever he's told you, it's bollocks. I swear, it's bollocks."

Morrison lurked in the doorway to the kitchen. "Where's the money, Pickett?"

"What money?"

Dylan had no patience for Pickett. He was a dirty rent boy who should be grateful. Most little shits in his line of work lived on the street. They'd sheltered him, given him a safe place to sleep in exchange for a fair share of the profits, and because Pickett—who was nineteen or twenty—looked about thirteen years old, there was always plenty of profit. Dylan didn't take any joy in hurting skinny weaklings, especially if they'd never raised a hand to him first, so he gave the scrote one last chance.

"Truth or dare?"

Pickett stopped squirming and looked up. He had a sore on his mouth and what was either terrible acne or a suspicious-looking rash across one side of his face and down his neck. "Huh?"

Dylan repeated himself, more slowly this time. "Truth or dare? Truth, you tell me where the money is, or dare, you pull out one of your teeth with these."

He slammed a pair of pliers on the kitchen table so hard that Pickett jumped in his seat and let out a squeal like a rusty hinge. "Nee way. Come on, Dylan, I didn't take any money. I didn't. I didn't."

He started to cry. Man, he hated it when they cried. The criers reminded him of himself when he was seven or eight, when the other kids would form a circle around him in the schoolyard and take turns spitting on the weird-looking kid. Dylan knew what was at stake here. Morrison was a capo and wouldn't usually concern himself with these matters. He should have left it with Hurls to divvy it out to one associate or another. Still, Morrison—one level down from Fletcher—had told Hurls to tell Dylan. It was a test; Dylan had to show strength. He had to show he was unflappable and capable of handling anything. He was Fletcher Blackburn's eldest son and the throne should go to him. He'd fucking earned it, unlike Theo, who caused nothing but trouble. He had to show he was a leader before this whole enterprise went to shit.

"Don't want to play truth or dare, Pickett? That's fine, you can take the forfeit instead."

"Nah, nah. Dylan, listen... Listen, mate—"

"I'm not your mate."

"Sorry. Sorry, Dylan." He tried to hold up his hands to apologise, but because of the rope, couldn't lift them more than a centimetre from his thighs. "It's not that I don't want to play. Truth. I pick truth."

Dylan scraped a second chair across the linoleum floor and sat facing the thin, frightened man. "All right." Dylan leant in so that his face was less than three inches from Pickett's and yelled, "WHERE IS THE MONEY?"

More tears ran down his face. "There is no money. I haven't been lifting. That's the truth, Dylan. That's the truth. Hurls has just got it in for me."

Dylan could feel the rage building as it had done so many times before. He struggled to keep it at a simmer. "I'd think carefully about insulting someone like Hurls."

He couldn't kill him. Well, he could—easily. But dissolving their under-sized earner isna vat of hydrofluoric acid wouldn't get them their money back, and it would cut their future income.

"I wasn't insulting him. I was just—"

Dylan looked at Morrison. He didn't look impressed. *Shit*. It was time to get serious.

"Just nothing," Dylan growled. "I've had enough. You get the forfeit. Time to say goodbye to your legs."

He stood, grabbed both of Pickett's legs and placed his feet on the chair from which he'd just stood. He raised his own foot and hovered it above Pickett's left knee joint.

"No, no, no, no, no, no. Not my legs. Please, please, I need my legs."

Tears flooded from his eyes.

"You're a fucking low life, addict, rent boy. You don't need legs; you only need your gob and your arse."

Dylan stomped his leg downwards. Through the thick soles of his boot, he still felt the snapping of Pickett's fibula and tibia.

The scream that followed was bound to trigger a migraine; it would kick in in an hour or two. It was a good thing they'd soundproofed this place.

Saliva poured from Pickett's open mouth as he writhed in the chair. Dylan raised his foot again, this time hovering it over his right leg.

"WAIT," he bellowed, closing his eyes. "Under... the bed... Loose floorboard."

Bingo.

Dylan kept his leg raised and primed while Morrison went to check. When he returned, he was waving a wad of cash.

"Three g's."

Dylan placed his foot back on the floor and looked down on the snivelling thief.

"Please... I need an ambulance."

Morrison had barely taken his phone from his pocket when Dylan slapped it from his hand. The phone skidded across the dirty floor and came to a stop by an overflowing bin. Morrison looked like his spleen was ready to blow.

"We need the lad fixing up so he can see punters again," he growled.

"You mental? Bringing the flashing blue lights round here?"

"I was going to leave him in the street," Morrison said through clenched teeth.

Dylan walked right up to Morrison and towered over him. "Still too close for comfort. Drop him by the phone box in the park." He pushed past him. "And have someone follow him to the hospital. Make sure he doesn't nick off."

Dylan needed to get home and take a beta-blocker before his vision started to cloud, but despite his sore head, Dylan smiled as he strode away. He'd just given a capo an order. What did that make him?

In another area of Newcastle, Aleksei Pavlovich unlocked Vixen. He deactivated the gentlemen's club's alarm system and picked up his post from the doormat. He shuffled the letters together into a neat pile and thumbed through them one by one. Electric bill, tax demand, flyer for Indian food, bank statement and, oh joy, a letter from the water company to say his rates were going up. Again.

Aleksei switched on the lights and shielded his eyes as the bulbs stuttered and flickered into life. What had become of his baby? His club had been the talk of the town when he opened in 1995. Lawyers brought clients here for a light lunch, to butter them up and seal the deal. Accountants came after work to celebrate having saved their bosses millions by making a thousand hard-working, blue-collar guys redundant. Footballers came to throw their money around and party the night away. He had the prettiest girls in town and the money they attracted meant Aleksei had been able to buy the most exquisite things for the club. It had been opulent. Now, his baby was depressed, like a faded photograph or a wilting flower. It made him sad just to be there. Lad culture was discouraged in big businesses; shareholders had no interest in indiscretions that could land their firm on the wrong side of a Twitter mob. And the footballers stayed away, instead choosing to spend time with their families. What was the world coming to?

Aleksei opened the dishwasher and found two glasses hadn't survived the wash cycle. *Wonderful. More things that need replacing.* There'd been a leak in the bathroom for three weeks now, and he couldn't afford a plumber. His favourite blonde had quit after getting herself pregnant, the graceful brunette with legs up to her armpits hadn't shown up in days, he was behind on his car payments and he was sure one of the bouncers had his fingers in the till. And now, to top it off, Fletcher Blackburn was dead.

Aleksei was no fan of Fletcher Blackburn, nor was he a fan of his ogreish son. Coming round every month demanding their *pizzo*. That's what the Italians call it: a *pizzo*. Aleksei called it extortion. At least Fletcher had been consistent, the pizzo hadn't been raised since the turn of the millennium. Just shy of a monkey each and every month. Four hundred and fifty fucking quid. It was money Aleksei could have used to fix the leak, to pay his car off, to put towards his mounting credit card debt. Now Fletcher was gone Aleksei was worried about who would take his place, because someone would definitely take his place. And when they did, how much would the pizzo be then?

There was a noise in the back alley. The damn cat must have got in the bins again. He thumbed through the pile of letters once more and let out a long sigh at his electric bill. Choosing the ostrich approach of burying his head in the sand, Aleksei dropped the pile of letters in the bin. They could wait until next month's reminder.

Years ago, Aleksei had tried to rally the other bar, club and restaurant owners in this and the surrounding streets. He'd heard of the *addiopizzo* movement in Sicily and hoped to start something similar in Newcastle. A union of sorts. But people were nervous about going against the Blackburns. Venues had been trashed for refusal to pay, people had been hurt, maybe even killed. Aleksei poured himself an apple juice and leant over to rest his head on the bar; it smelled of cleaning products. Perhaps, now that Fletcher was dead, it would be a good time to try and form his *addiopizzo* union again. He closed his eyes and wondered if such a thing could work on Tyneside, then he was distracted by another noise.

Aleksei froze, focusing his hearing towards the dressing room that the girls used. There was a rustling and a crackling, followed by a whooshing noise. It wasn't the damn cat, and it wasn't in the back alley.

- Chapter 23 -

Forensics thought they'd collected all they needed from the Blackburns' home in rural Northumberland, but given the news about Fletcher's digoxin poisoning, they pulled their bunny suits back on and scattered themselves around the grounds of the manor home in search of more clues. With the SOCOs dressed in identical white all-in-ones, complete with hoods and boots, it was impossible to distinguish one from the other. Atkinson could be any of them. Cooper had her team record their attendance in the crime scene log book, then they pulled on their own PPE to protect the scene and got to work looking for handwriting samples. The grounds, study and kitchen were bustling with activity, so they began upstairs in the bedrooms.

"This is the master bedroom," Cooper said, pushing open a heavy, solid wood door. It was exactly how they had left it on Tuesday. That was only two days ago and yet so much had happened. It was one of those weeks when you were so busy that time slipped away from you and days ended before you even felt like they had begun and yet the week passed at a snail's pace. Despite the slow pace, Cooper loved the hunt, not in the visceral way that Keaton loved it, but in the problem-solving sense. This was a logic puzzle that needed to be unlocked. Unfortunately, as much as Cooper wanted to see the case through to the end, there was the matter of her father and her need to see him as soon as possible. When Ben Cooper came out of surgery, he'd be kept in intensive care, be monitored for arrhythmia and pumped full of drugs to thin his blood. Part of her craved stability. Wouldn't it be nice to have the sort of job where you could take leave whenever it was required? To work the same hours each day, knowing exactly what was expected of you and what needed doing for each shift? *No,* she thought, stopping by the dresser drawer where Hong Evanstad had found Fletcher's gun. *Absolutely not.*

Unable to do anything for Ben right now, Cooper turned her attention back to the search. "Anything with handwriting on it is useful," Cooper told the team. "This is the room Charlene shared with Fletcher. We've removed Charlene from our list of most likely suspects based on her height and the evidence from our hired help from Greater Manchester, but let's be thorough. Find something she wrote just to back that up."

Tennessee took a sniff of the wine glass that had been abandoned on the bedside table and wrinkled his nose. "Smells like vinegar." He picked up a romance novel with a fancy lace bookmark hanging from it and read the title. "Summer in Sicily: A Mobster Romance? I guess Charlene Blackburn has a type."

Keaton suppressed a laugh. "My mum used to read that type of book. Western romance, billionaire romance, bad boy romance, reverse harem. You name it, it's out there."

"What the hell's reverse harem?" Martin pulled a spiral-bound notepad out of a junk drawer and flicked through the lined pages. "Blank," he added.

Keaton found an old Valentine's card in a shoebox at the back of Fletcher's wardrobe. "One woman, lots of boyfriends. What other books does she have over there?"

Tennessee put *Summer in Sicily* back down on the bedside table."She has eclectic tastes. There's Hemingway, Wilde, a Stephen King novella and... Oh, what do we have here? *Gardening Through the Year*."

Cooper looked over. "George told us Charlene was redesigning the garden."

"You don't need to be six-foot-two to poison someone," Tennessee added. "Maybe Charlene stumbled across toxic plants during her research. We might have been too quick in releasing her."

"You're right." Cooper took the book as evidence. "But let's stay on track for now. I want handwriting samples."

Keaton handed the Valentine's card she found to Cooper, who examined the pink, glittery writing.

"*I love you with all my heart*...Looped tails here on the Y of *you* and again on the Y of *my*."

"Different structure overall though," Keaton said. "Too round compared to the diary entry." She held a copy of the page in question. "This is more oval based and very slanted. Like it's written in italics."

Cooper agreed. The two samples were very different. "Shall we move on?" The team followed her from the master bedroom, past a bathroom and a home gym, to the next room along the hallway. She stopped to check a room plan from her file. "This should be Dylan's room." She entered and cast her gaze around. "Now before any of you smart arses make a joke about Dylan Blackburn not being able to read or write, remember looks can be deceiving. Charlene told us people assumed he was slow, but we all know what happens when you assume things."

Tennessee nodded. "It makes an *ass of you and me*... It's like an opium den in here. Blinds closed, curtains closed, low watt bulb."

"He suffers from migraines. It probably helped to keep his room in darkness." Cooper began to work her way through the room. She watched Keaton open the wardrobe and drawers and noted the amount of camo print clothing he had. What struck Cooper most was how little the room told her about Dylan. There was no indication of who he was as a person; no photographs of loved ones, no signs of a hobby, no books or DVDs. Not that anyone bought DVDs these days, she corrected herself. Dylan's room appeared to be a functional space for sleeping and dressing, nothing more. All the surfaces were clean and dust-free, and nothing was strewn about. The only sign of life was a dehydrated peace lily in a terracotta pot. Had the nuns beaten this level of discipline into him?

"I've got something," Martin said, holding a scrap of paper. "A phone number. Doesn't say whose it is."

Cooper took it and they continued their search, finally finding a sudoku book tucked under Dylan's pillow.

Keaton opened the puzzle book and pulled a face. She scanned through a few more pages and pulled an even stranger face.

"What is it?" Cooper asked.

"I've never been able to finish these bastards. Could never get my head around them. But this son of a bitch has finished loads of them. In fact, I can't find a single one that he's started and not finished. You might be right about looks being deceptive, boss."

Cooper chuckled as she took the sudoku book. "What me?" she said sarcastically. "Be right about something? Never in the world."

The room next door belonged to George Blackburn, and it couldn't have been further in style to that of his brother's. Whilst it was also impeccably clean with no sign of mess, the room was warm and bright, decorated in shades of white, stone and cornflour blue. It reminded Cooper of a boutique hotel with its floor-length curtains and reading chair by the window. George was an avid reader by the looks of his bookshelves. A quick look in his desk drawer told her he was into art: a set of watercolour pencils, a putty rubber, and a pad of artist's paper.

"Bless, he still keeps his pyjamas under his pillow," Keaton joked as she checked around the bed.

Martin frowned. "Doesn't everyone do that?"

The team stopped to stare at him.

"That's where my mum puts them when they've been ironed—" he stopped himself too late. "I'm not going to live that down, am I?"

Keaton shook her head and patted him on the back. "Not for a long time, kiddo."

"Well, well, well," Tennessee said, bringing their focus back to the investigation. No shortage of handwriting samples for Georgie Boy. He's an aspiring poet." Tennessee held up a satin-backed notepad that he'd recovered from the bookshelf. "Listen to this... *Golden hair and aqua eyes, angel wings and butterflies. Gentle soul with slender wrists, she fears the man and fears his fists. Angel run away, fly free, angel run away with me.*" He blew a raspberry. "Blimey. That apple fell a long way from the tree."

Cooper tried not to giggle as she took the book of poems. This was George baring his soul, something he probably couldn't do verbally with a family such as his. Cooper wondered if he'd ever shared his love of art or poetry with any of his family. If he had, he'd probably been mocked for it. "Oval structure," she mused as she examined the shapes of the letters. "What do you think?" she asked, showing the book to Keaton.

Keaton squinted and gave Cooper a subtle nod.

Five minutes later and they were in a lilac-coloured, princess-themed room complete with crystal chandelier, four-poster bed and a dresser that housed more make-up than a branch of Boots. The name Lily was written in fairy lights across a wall, and stuffed toys, mostly pink, peered at Cooper from a window seat.

"Let's find a diary or something sharpish," Cooper said. "Those cuddly bears are giving me the creeps. I feel like they're watching me."

It was a feeling Cooper was experiencing more and more. Every button, bulb or bubble could be a hidden camera as far as she was concerned.

"This whole room gives me the creeps," Tennessee added. "I feel like if I stay in here too long, I'll need testosterone replacement therapy."

"I thought Hayley painted Alfie's room purple?" Cooper asked.

"She did," said Tennessee, "but the decorating fairy turned up one night and painted it blue."

Cooper snorted as she opened Lily's wardrobe and examined her designer handbags. "Does the decorating fairy have blond curls and a Geordie accent by any chance?"

He grinned at her. "Ah divint knaa what ya on aboot, pet."

"Bingo." Martin had a notepad in his gloved hand. "Looks like handwritten notes on gel versus acrylic manicures."

"Excellent. That should do it." Cooper let her eyes float over the rest of Lily's wardrobe and her expansive shoe collection. Cooper's black boots with sturdy soles were boring and androgynous in comparison to the array of shoes on display. Jewel encrusted ballerina shoes, stylish court shoes,

shoes with see-through heels, shoes with glittered soles, pink trainers and designer flip-flops.

"Erica?...ERICA?"

Justin Atkinson's voice was tense and urgent. It caught her completely by surprise. "We're up here," she called, leaving the room to peer over the bannister.

Atkinson pulled his hood down and removed his protective mask. "Erm... The television in the lounge is on." He thumbed towards one of the downstairs rooms. "One of the guys wanted to check last night's footie scores..." He shrugged and rolled his eyes. "Anyway, the news is on. You should come down and see for yourself."

The scene reminded Cooper of earlier that morning when everyone had huddled around Keaton's desk. Now the SOCOs had gathered around the television in a semicircle, a hum of shocked chatter drowning out the news presenter's voice.

"Quiet." Cooper's solitary word did its job, and the wall of white fell into silence.

The studio cut to Newcastle city centre where a glossy-lipped correspondent addressed the camera. "Shocking scenes in Newcastle today as firefighters struggle to control fires at three bars. The western end of Westgate Road, the Cloth Market and Stepney Lane have all been evacuated."

"Jesus," Keaton muttered. "What's going on?"

"My eyes are stinging from smoke," the correspondent continued. "We're being asked to vacate the area. You can see behind me that the sky, which was cloudless only half an hour ago is now black with smoke. I... Yes, we'll move in two minutes... We're live on air... Authorities have confirmed that the fires started in McDermott's, The Silver Mirror and Vixen. Back to the studio."

Cooper switched the television off. "Everyone back to work."

Once the bunny suits disbanded, she turned to Tennessee, Martin and Keaton. "They're all Blackburn controlled bars. Shit. This is heavy. It's broad daylight."

"Hanson?" Tennessee asked.

"Of course it's Hanson. Get onto Whyte and Boyd. Find out what they know and see if the phone company has got back to Boyd yet. Martin, have someone protect the daughter at the RVI. The Blackburns *will* retaliate."

Tennessee wiped his face nervously. "Eddie has a lot of contacts. Between him and Dylan, I think they'll blow up half of Gateshead if they think they need to."

Cooper looked to the floor to gather herself. It was all going to shit. On her watch. "I know. That's what I'm afraid of."

- Chapter 24 -

Justin Atkinson had stopped to smell the roses. Literally. Cooper observed him double over, stick his nose in the rose bushes and inhale deeply. Next to him, an old yew blackened from a lightning strike was struggling to hold on. Patches of green spine-shaped leaves grew on the branches that hadn't been damaged, and the sun filtered through, speckling the lawn and flowerbeds with dots of light and shade. Cooper's phone vibrated; she removed it from her pocket to look at the screen. It was Olly Timms asking if she'd eaten yet because he was near Wallsend and could bring her some lunch. No, she hadn't eaten yet, the rumbling in her stomach confirmed that, but she was also nowhere near HQ and she was staring at the man she really wanted to have lunch with.

Right on cue, Atkinson looked up. Cooper hastily shoved her phone back in her pocket, pulled her shoulders back and flashed a smile.

He nodded his head towards another flowerbed, and they ambled towards it, their steps in sync with one another. In a parallel universe, Cooper and Atkinson would be hand-in-hand, walking through the manicured grounds of a different stately home. Belsay Hall, Longframlington Gardens, it wouldn't matter as long as they were together. Instead, they were walking at a respectful distance from one another, through the scene of a double murder.

"The foxgloves are over here," Atkinson told her.

"They're pretty," Cooper commented as she looked at the spires of purple and white bell-shaped flowers that reached for the sky.

"Pretty, but deadly," he smiled, "I've known a few women who can go by that description."

Cooper looked away. "It's definitely the nicest murder weapon I've seen. Any chance you can lift prints from the flower petals?"

"It hasn't rained, so yes, there is a small chance. It'll be difficult, but I'll try. That's assuming our killer wasn't wearing gardening gloves. You can see here that this plant has been pruned recently." He pointed to where a stem had been clipped and leaves removed.

"So Ronnie's gone back to Manchester?"

"Yes, she headed back this morning. What a talent. Watching her work was really something."

"Are you going to visit her?"

Atkinson looked confused. "Why would I do that?"

Cooper lifted her shoulders and put her hands in her pockets. "Because you seemed to hit it off."

"Well, she is great, and we have a lot in common, but I'm not looking for a long-distance thing."

The warmth of the sun felt good on Cooper's skin. She pushed the sleeves of her shirt up so her forearms could benefit too.

"Manchester's only three hours away," she said before she could stop herself. What was she doing? If Cooper could have slapped herself, she would've done.

"Why would I want a long-distance relationship when the perfect woman lives a ten-minute walk from my house?"

Hopes dashed, Cooper had to accept that Atkinson had moved on. She could hardly blame him. She began to pick at the skin around her thumbnail until a lightbulb slowly illuminated in the darkest corner of her mind. Didn't *she* live a ten-minute walk from Atkinson's house?

"Me?"

"Yes, you." He laughed. "It's always been you."

Cooper didn't know quite what to do. She had hurt him terribly; she'd pushed him away when all he was trying to do was keep her safe. "I'm far from perfect," she mumbled.

"That's the thing about perfection," he said, picking a snapdragon from the flowerbed and handing it to Cooper, "like the beauty of a flower, it belongs entirely in the eye of the beholder."

Before Cooper could ask him to dinner, or simply extend her arm and stroke her hand against his, she spotted Keaton moving quickly in their direction.

"Coop, the fire at McDermott's has been extinguished. No casualties. The Silver Mirror is under control, and three people have been transferred to the RVI due to smoke inhalation."

"Thanks, Paula. What about Vixen?"

"They're struggling to contain it. Some sort of accelerant has been used—probably petrol. It's spreading to the office building next door." She paused and looked back and forth between Cooper and Atkinson. "Everything okay? You look weird, boss."

Cooper hoped that if she was blushing she could at least pass it off as sunburn. "I'm fine. What's the consensus on the handwriting samples? Are we all in agreement?"

"We are, and if I'm being honest, I'm not shocked."

Atkinson clapped his hands together. "You have a theory?"

The right corner of Cooper's mouth turned upwards, and she popped her hands on her hips. "I do. I just need more evidence. Which is where you two come in. Paula, can you find out where the three nearest libraries are and pay them a visit? I want to know what books the Blackburns have been checking out. If they haven't been using their laptops or phones, they've been getting their research from somewhere."

Keaton nodded and walked away, calling over her shoulder, "Consider it done."

Checking to make sure no one was around, Cooper moved closer to Atkinson and let her little finger brush against his forearm.

He sighed. "I really want to kiss you right now."

Cooper's stomach flipped over, and she gave him a coquettish look.

"And we have a lot to talk about," he added.

He was right. There were reasons beyond Kenny Roberts that had caused her and Atkinson problems. Kenny had just been the tinderbox. "We can talk... and kiss, as much as we like, but only once this case is out of the way," she teased. "Right now, I need you to test the following items from the kitchen, office and bedrooms..."

THE INFERNO HAD SPREAD to a pair of offices above Vixen. The sky was stained a dark grey, and tiny, ashy, scraps of paper floated towards the pavement like paper raindrops. It reminded Watch Manager Jed Coles of a show he'd watched about Chernobyl; thankfully, nothing here was radioactive. Now that the orange flickers and popping noises had subsided, the crowds had thinned and dispersed, only a few nosy buggers remained. One of his men emerged from the strip joint and began to remove his breathing apparatus. Even in full gear, Coles knew he was looking at Pinkman. He could recognise all of blue watch by either their frame, posture or gait.

"It's out, gaffer," Pinkman said. "Was a right ball ache getting it under control. Fucker poured petrol all round the back before setting the place alight.

When the flames reached the bar, the alcohol only worsened it."

"And the two on the stairs?"

"The smoke got them before the flames. Poor bastards must have panicked, forgot about the external fire escape and tried to come out the front entrance. The stairwell's above the bar area; it was thick with smoke. Would've been disorientating."

Cole ran a hand over the back of his neck. Usually, commercial fires were easier to deal with than residential fires, emotionally speaking at least. You didn't have to sift through the charred remnants of a family's possessions: cherished memories, photos from once in a lifetime holidays, portraits of departed loved ones, baby teeth, locks of hair and ticket stubs from first dates to the cinema. But bodies were bodies. Didn't matter if they were in a home or a business—they were never easy to deal with. Two people had gone to work this morning and would never return home.

"Thanks, Pinkman," Coles said. "Give the station manager a bell and update him."

"Aye," he replied.

"And thank the crews from Byker for their assistance," Coles added. Central had been unable to handle the three simultaneous fires on their own and crews from Byker and Gosforth had been called in to assist. "This was a tough one. Tell the lads I'll be in the Vic tonight if anyone fancies a pint."

Pinkman nodded and headed towards one of the engines. Across the road, a smallish woman with a slight frame and hair shorter than his was speaking to Gibson. She held up some form of ID and was allowed through the cordon.

"Watch Manager Coles? I'm—"

"DCI Cooper. Yes, I was expecting you. I'm afraid the situation has worsened."

"Really? I heard the fire had been extinguished."

"It has." Coles looked around and conducted a silent headcount of his men and women. He always wanted to know how many were in and out of a building at any one time. "But it was hard going, and it was definitely started deliberately. I have no doubt about that. Two fatalities and a casualty."

Coles watched Cooper's face. She had the same look he did when confronted with death. She was saddened. She didn't know the two people who had perished in the blaze, but it affected her all the same.

"No identification for the DBs yet, but I can tell you they were descending from the upstairs offices. The surviving casualty is the owner of the bar. He suffered burns and minor smoke inhalation. He's been taken to hospital as a precaution."

"Did he see the arsonist?"

Coles shook his head. "Not really. Saw the back of his head as he legged it out the back door into the alley. Male. Medium height. Medium build. Brown hair."

"That narrows it down," Cooper said with dry sarcasm. She folded her arms over her chest. "I'll find out if there are any cameras covering the back lane, but I imagine it's just a waiting game until the investigation team can tell us more."

Coles smiled.

"What?" She asked, her eyes narrowing.

"Follow me." Coles strode away at a quick pace, forcing the shorter woman to practically break into a jog to keep up with him. He turned when he reached the end of the street where tents for collecting evidence were already erected. Coles stuck his head into the first tent and emerged seconds later with a clear plastic evidence bag. "Thought this might come in useful."

COOPER COULD HAVE HUGGED him. "Where was it found?"

"In the back alley. It was dropped by our medium-height, medium-build male."

Cooper clasped her hands together as if thanking a deity. Sometimes the CID gods threw her a bone, and today's bone was shaped like a Google Pixel XL mobile phone. With Atkinson busy in the lab and Keaton traversing between rural libraries, Cooper finally had something tangible, something she could grasp with two hands and present as evidence.

"You're a star."

Coles shrugged sheepishly. "It's likely a burner. Pardon the pun."

"It's a pretty swanky phone for a burner. I'll get it straight to our tech team. If there's a trail, they'll find it."

Cooper high-tailed it the short journey to Byker Police Station where the digital forensics lab was located and handed the clear evidence bag to Rebecca Hogg. Rebecca Hogg was affectionately known as Becky the Techie and whilst she might look innocent enough in her beanie hat, large, wire-framed glasses and oversized jumper, rumour had it she also had two side hustles on the go. She was both a qualified skydiving instructor and was selling her urine over the internet. Some people might want clean urine to pass mandatory work-place drug tests, but others just liked buying pee from young women. It took all sorts.

Within ten minutes, Becky had already confirmed that the phone was registered as stolen and that our genius arsonist hadn't been too careful.

"He signs his texts as JR," Becky told her. She kept scrolling. "Has a girlfriend by the looks of it... Oh, here we go, she calls him Johnny."

"Surname?"

She pushed her glasses up until they rested on top of her grey beanie. "Not that I can see. Leave it with me. I'll run some programmes and see what I can come up with. Pop back in an hour?"

Cooper thanked Becky and decided to use her hour to tidy up a bit of home admin. She walked the short distance to Morrisons and picked up a few staples as her cupboards were looking worryingly bare. She got pasta, rice, tinned tomatoes, tinned fish and other basics that most people always had in, as well as sunscreen, insect repellant and some new razors. When queuing for the checkout, she called her mother. No answer.

Once her shopping had been deposited in the BMW's boot, Cooper used her remaining time to check the flight schedule between Newcastle International and Lanzarote. The next flight wasn't until Sunday, meaning she had no choice but to swim in Saturday's triathlon.

"Tell me you have a name," Cooper pleaded when she returned to Becky the Techie's desk.

Beckie took a long slurp from a KFC drink and kept drinking until the gurgling noise indicated the cup was empty. "You want the good news, the really good news, or the *really really* good news?"

"The good news first."

"I have a name: Johnathon R. Kane. Here's his email."

"And the really good news?" Cooper asked.

"I know what he looks like. Here's a selfie he took just last week."

Cooper drew back in horror. "A trigger warning would have been nice."

Beckie laughed. "Sorry. Here's one where he's wearing clothes."

Cooper concluded that like detectives, digital forensic technicians probably had a sick sense of humour. When half their job entailed finding evidence of child abuse, if the techies didn't know how to make a joke every now and again, they'd go crazy.

"This is better," Cooper said, holding the printout Beckie had given her. "And dare I ask, what's the *really really* good news?"

"Genius Johnny didn't fully disable location services."

"Meaning?"

"Meaning I've looked for patterns and clusters in his location history and I can tell you exactly where he'll be tonight."

- Chapter 25 -

Two o'clock had been and gone before Cooper had her first meal of the day. There was a canteen and a host of vending machines to choose from at HQ, but craving some peace and quiet, the team took a short drive to the Shiremoor House Farm, a pub less than three minutes away by car. Almost seventy-two hours had passed since the shooting of Fletcher Blackburn and Ibrahim Moradi, and CID was a rat's nest of pandemonium. After the escalation in violence between those loyal to Blackburn and Hanson, Nixon had put out an appeal to the public and calls were coming into the hotline faster than they could be answered. Officers were busy sifting through the bullshit in the hope of finding something useful. Sadly, the public didn't grasp that the police only wanted information concerning the shootings at Morshaw Manor and the arson attacks in the city centre; they had little interest in the he-deserves-its and the

I-knew-he-was-troubles. Alibis had to be checked and double-checked. Everyone in the inner circle, apart from Dylan and Theo, had a reasonable to good alibi for the time of the murder. Dylan had, by his own admission, been tucked up in bed since lunchtime. It seemed ridiculous to Cooper, but if he were guilty, wouldn't he have thought of a better lie to spin than that? Theo was annoyingly allusive, only giving up that he was in both Newcastle and Sunderland that day. They'd yet to find CCTV footage of him on the Metro, and he'd given them no indication as to what he'd been up to or who he'd met when he'd got there. There was a chance he'd gone behind his uncle's back to meet with the Roker Boys, but in doing so, he'd also have gone against his father's wishes. No wonder he didn't want Cooper to speak to Eddie.

Tennessee went to the bar and ordered her a half pint of IPA and a bowl of cheesy chips. Cooper found a seat and took a moment to zone out and calm her mind. She breathed slowly and pictured a circle expanding and contracting in time with each breath, just as the mindfulness app had taught her during chemo. By the time Tennessee joined her, she'd managed to stave off the headache that had been threatening her since she saw the news that morning.

Full of fats and carbs, Cooper felt better as she walked back into Northumbria Police HQ. Tennessee had scoffed not only a plate of fish and chips but also a chicken parmo under the guise of carb-loading for the relay triathlon. Back in CID, Cooper cleared the incident room; she and Tennessee had calls to make, and they wanted some space to work without the current volume levels.

"I'll start with Rose Watson. Can you call the beauticians?"

Tennessee affirmed and opened a file to find the number he was after.

"Rose? Hello. This is DCI Erica Cooper from Northumbria Police. Sorry to disturb you but I wanted to ask you a few questions about a date you had with George Blackburn on the seventeenth of June?"

Rose was silent.

"Have you spoken to George since Monday?"

"No. What's this about? Did something happen to George?" Rose had a soft, child-like tone to her voice.

"George's father was shot that day."

There was a gasp. "Oh. Wow. I don't know what to say. I mean, I hardly knew George. We met online. But still, that's terrible."

Cooper quickly glanced over the report Keaton had given her. She could see Wagamama's had CCTV footage of George and Rose entering the restaurant at quarter past three, and Cineworld had confirmed they attended the half four showing of the latest Tarantino flick. "George told me he met you at two o'clock on Monday afternoon—" She was about to ask where the pair had been between two and quarter past three when Rose cut her off.

"No. That's not right."

"It's not?"

"No. We were supposed to meet at two, but George was late. I waited for ten minutes and decided to go shopping. I popped into Waterstones and got a couple of books then went to French Connection. He eventually showed up at three."

Cooper was taken aback. "He was an hour late?"

"Yeah." She sighed. "It was a nice date in the end, but I wasn't sure if I'd want a second one. I was pretty miffed at being kept waiting so long, and to be honest, I don't think he was that into me."

"Just one more thing, Rose. What was George like that afternoon? Can you tell me anything about his behaviour?"

"He was fine. A little quiet, I suppose, but he had perfect manners, other than being late. Wait. Why would you ask that? You want to know if he seemed shifty, don't you?"

Cooper had a feeling Rose was going to want a second date after all. In Rose's mind, George had gone from being a quiet gentleman, to a damaged boy who'd lost his father, to a potential murderer in the space of a brief conversation. Some girls couldn't resist a project; other girls couldn't resist a bad boy—someone who would change if only you could love them enough. Cooper wanted to tell her to run for the hills and stay as far from the Blackburns as she could, but alas, it was none of her business. She thanked Rose, hung up and turned to Tennessee. He was sat with his arms folded over his chest.

"George was an hour late," she told him. "So, he has no alibi until three o'clock. Not two o'clock like he told us."

"And get this. Martin spoke to a temp when he called in at the beauticians. She told him Lily had been scheduled to work that day, she was on the rota..."

"But?"

"But, I just spoke to the boss, and she told me Lily only popped in to get her legs and bikini line waxed. She'd actually swapped shifts with another girl. Said she'd told them she had somewhere else she needed to be."

Cooper was incensed. "This entire family is made up of liars and people who don't care if they look guilty. I should lock up every last one of them."

"Please do," Tennessee said. He raked his fingers through his curls and gave himself a brief head massage, his eyes closed as he processed things.

What Cooper wouldn't give for a massage right now.

"Right, let me get this straight," he continued. "We have two bodies at Morshaw and two bodies in Frankland. That's four murders and one attempted murder if you count Fletcher's poisoning."

"Which we do," Cooper added. "Plus we have three arson attacks and two people who died in the fire at Vixen."

"Charlene is too short to carry out the shooting, but she knows her way around a garden and would have known foxgloves were poisonous. Then there's George, who wasn't where he said he was, and Lily, who wasn't where she said she was. There's Dylan, who lied about knowing about the gun and has no alibi. And Theo, who won't give us a bloody alibi. Not a good one anyway."

"And Hanson who has way too much of an alibi," Cooper chimed in. "That's six suspects with six motives. They all stood to gain from killing Fletcher. Charlene gets money, yes she already had money, but not like this. Hanson would get power. With Fletcher and Eddie out of the way, I'm not sure the youngsters have enough clout with the soldiers to keep them onside. They'll desert a sinking ship and go work for Hanson or the Daytons or the blooming Roker Boys."

"Dylan's motive is revenge," said Tennessee. "What his parents put him through... I'd be surprised if he didn't off the mother as well. Lily gets the freedom to see who she wants, even if it is that arsehole cousin of hers."

"And that leaves George, who gets justice for the people he cares about, and Theo, who gets the keys to the Blackburn empire. But like I said, if he can hang on to it remains to be seen."

Tennessee got to his feet and bent over to stretch his back. "Sex and money," he mused. "It always comes down to sex and money. Six suspects, six motives. We may as well roll a dice and choose one." He straightened up and began stretching sideways.

Cooper laughed. "You think I need to roll a dice to solve this one?"

He met her gaze. "You said you were going to have to lock them all up."

"No. I said I *should* lock them all up. I have my favourites. I just need to hear from Keaton." Cooper's phone began vibrating. "Speak of the devil."

"You won't be calling me the devil when I tell you what I've got," Keaton answered.

"Hang on, I'll stick you on speaker phone. Okay, go."

"I'm in the bustling metropolis of Wooler," she said sarcastically.

Wooler was a small town in Northumberland with pretty stone buildings and the beautiful backdrop of the Cheviot hills.

"Two books were checked out of Wooler library on June the sixth and returned on June eleventh: Death In The Garden and Plants That Kill."

"Who checked them out?" Cooper asked.

"That would be our good friend Theo Blackburn."

"Theo?" *Interesting.*

Tennessee pointed at her and mouthed, *Told you so. Sex and money.*

"Confirm with CCTV, Paula, and see what else is on his reading list of late. Get ahold of the books as well. I want them in the lab tonight. If someone else has checked them out, find them."

Cooper hung up and called Atkinson.

"Hey beautiful," he whispered.

"Hey you." She could hardly say *Hey handsome* with Tennessee sat next to her. Not that it mattered, he was making kissy faces anyway. Cooper covered the receiver and hissed at her DS, "Remember what I said about transferring you to Sunderland?"

Tennessee held his hands up in defeat.

"Make yourself useful and go and check the start times for that stupid triathlon thing... Okay, Justin, give me some good news."

"I tested the item you were interested in. Trace evidence of digoxin."

Cooper punched the air. "Yes! Paula will be bringing some books your way. Death In The Garden and Plants That Kill. I need to know whose prints are on what pages."

"That sounds time consuming."

"But you'll do it for me, right?"

"Well, as it's you... Anything else I can do for the great DCI Erica Cooper?"

"Yes." Cooper had checked the flight schedule between Newcastle International and Lanzarote and knew she wouldn't be able to see her father until Sunday afternoon at the earliest. She planned on using her time between then and now as best she could by not only solving the Blackburn case, but by winning back Atkinson. With the spirit of *who dares, wins*, she asked the burning question.

"Will you have dinner with me on Saturday night?" Cooper held her breath while she waited for the answer. It may be too soon and asking him the second Ronnie left the region was probably a touch desperate, but she hadn't been able to help herself. He hadn't answered yet. Why hadn't he answered yet? The pause went on and on, and when he finally responded, his voice was trembly.

"I'd love to."

Thank god.

"But on one condition. I cook. No offence but—"

Cooper's insides were dancing. "I know, I know... I can burn water."

KEATON STRUGGLED TO GET comfortable on a swivel chair as she watched and rewatched a segment of CCTV footage. The armrests of the chair dug into her thighs and pinched her glutes. It must have been made for a child or one of those eight-stone, size six women she wanted to force-feed. That, or Keaton had been overdoing the squats of late. Nonsense. There was no such thing as too many squats. She scooted her weight to the left and almost toppled the chair. Once her heart calmed down, she rewound the footage and watched it again.

She was watching Theo Blackburn walk into the library, browse the science aisles, select a number of books, flick through them, choose two and check them out. She rubbed her eyes and moved her face closer to the screen. He was the right height and build, but the baseball cap he wore was doing her head in; she didn't have a single second of footage with a clear view of his face. It was probably Theo, but she could just as easily be looking at Dylan or George. Heck, it could have been Fletcher himself. *No*, she thought to herself, *Fletcher wouldn't wear camo print shorts... But Dylan would.*

Dylan's wardrobe had been filled with camouflage print when she'd seen it as part of the search.

Had he taken Theo's library card? He could have done.

On the desk, a clear evidence bag contained a copy of Plants That Kill. The other book, Death In The Garden, had been checked out by someone who lived three streets away. She'd pay the elderly man a visit when she was done here and get both books to Justin. She wondered if it would be Theo or Dylan's prints he'd find.

Keaton squirmed. Unable to handle it any longer, she stood and slid the chair away. She retrieved a USB stick from her pocket and downloaded the video footage for Cooper to take a look at later. Next, she logged back into the library's system. Theo Blackburn's account was only two months old, and prior to that, he hadn't checked out a single book. Not surprising. He seemed the sort to watch Fast and Furious films on repeat. Chances were, he only set up the account so that he didn't have to look up information on poisons on his phone or laptop. She was about to log off when something caught her eye, and she scanned down the info attached to Theo's account. Slowly, very slowly, a huge grin spread across her face, and she laughed so loud a man in a tweed jacket hushed her.

"Sorry," Keaton whispered, though she wasn't sorry in the slightest. She hit the control and P keys on the computer's keyboard and waited while an ancient printer spewed up what she'd been looking at on the monitor. Still unable to stop smiling, Keaton called Cooper.

"Boss. The good news is that I've got one book in my possession and I know where the other one is. I'll have them both in the lab within an hour. Ninety minutes tops."

"And the bad news?"

"The CCTV system here is a bobby dazzler. Instant results and good quality footage. I have video of a man checking out the books in question. Same height and build as Theo but for two reasons I can't be one hundred per cent sure it's him. First, he's wearing a baseball cap that covers half his face. I don't have a single frame that we can realistically use."

"Shit."

"Don't despair," said Keaton with a teasing tone to her voice.

"Why?" asked Cooper. "What was the second reason?"

"His account was only set up two months ago. He registered online, and you'll never guess in a million years what his password is."

- Chapter 26 -

Cooper called Aleksei Pavlovich for the fifth time. There was one piece of information she needed to unravel this web of lies, and she was sure it lay in the hands of Vixen's owner. An off-hand remark by one of the younger Blackburns had niggled at the back of her brain for a while. Something had interfered with Fletcher's plans that day. There must have been a reason for him to go home after collecting his money from Vixen rather than moving onto McDermott's or Bambi Bar. The phone company had confirmed he hadn't received any calls during the timeframe they were looking at, so something had either angered him, scared him, or tempted him away. Cooper thought she knew which.

No answer. She tried again, this time leaving a disgruntled message about how she understood how busy he was, what with his bar burning to the ground, but if he didn't call her back within the hour someone would start checking visas.

Cooper then issued messages to the team that she wanted them all back at Northumbria Police Headquarters by nine p.m. for a meeting. When Elliot Whyte called asking if it couldn't wait until the morning briefing, she almost bit his head off.

"There isn't going to be a morning briefing, Elliot. Instructions tonight; action tomorrow. Be here at nine or don't be here at all."

There was silence on Whyte's end of the call. Cooper could picture him biting his tongue. "Ma'am," he said eventually with all the fake politeness in his voice that he could muster.

While Cooper waited, she checked on Tina who was alone and waiting for Josh to come over to do homework. Or, at least that's what she told her mother they were going to be doing.

"That's fine. No alcohol though."

Tina gave one of her trademark huffs before sulkily replying, "No, Mum. I told you, we're doing homework."

"I believe you, but put my mind at ease and tell me you've been taking your pill every morning."

"Oh, sweet baby seagulls! Yes, mum!"

"At the same time each day? Because if you take it late or—"

"Mum!"

Cooper stopped to laugh at herself. She didn't mean to hassle Tina. Her daughter had proven herself to be trustworthy and honest, but the higher Cooper's adrenaline levels climbed, the more she fixated on those she held dear. All she had ever wanted from the moment Tina was born was for her to have the chances Cooper had never had; for her to be sheltered from the side-glances and insults that had come Cooper's way when her baby bump had begun to show at such a young age.

"Sorry T. I'm a little on edge."

"You don't say."

Cooper ran a hand over her head to the back of her neck where she began massaging her trapezius muscles. Tina was very fond of her grandfather. Cooper wasn't sure how she'd react to the news of his heart attack. When she'd told her about her breast cancer diagnosis, Tina had clammed up and stopped talking for almost a month. Selective mutism was what the doctor called it. The shock and worry had overwhelmed her, and she'd been unable to express herself verbally. Knowing her mutism was causing her mother anxiety had only added to Tina's guilt and made the situation worse. Cooper had been forced to find a way to carry on as if everything was normal, including communicating through pen and paper, nods and shakes, thumbs up and thumbs down, until Tina could relax.

"I'm going to be late. It'll be at least ten when I get in." Cooper said. She'd have to tell Tina tonight and hoped some junk food would lessen the impact. "Fancy a late supper? I can bring in a takeaway?"

Tina didn't hesitate. "Salt and pepper ribs and duck in plum sauce."

"Okay. Stay safe and lock the doors."

Another huff.

Cooper got to her feet when the line went dead and wandered in search of coffee. *Sweet baby seagulls?* That was a new one. She opted for a black Americano from the vending machine. She almost dropped it on herself when Vixen's owner finally returned her call.

"Mr Pavlovich, I'm texting you a photograph. I want to know everything you know."

IT WAS GONE EIGHT when suspected arsonist Johnny R Kane was dragged into HQ. Becky the Techie had been right about his habits. She'd told Cooper he'd been in the Tanners Arms every Thursday night since he acquired the phone. The Tanners was a popular pub near Newcastle's train station. Cooper hadn't been in years, but she had fond memories of their Sunday lunch. According to Kane's data, Becky predicted he'd arrive between half-five and six and would stay until half-ten. Two of Whyte's contacts from Newcastle City Centre Police Station had picked him up just as he was about to tuck into a pie and a pint and brought him to Wallsend. SOCOs immediately took his prints and DNA as well as various swabs. They'd look for traces of accelerants and other evidence that he'd started the fires rather than just being in the wrong place at the wrong time.

By the time Cooper got her hands on him, it would be closer to eight-thirty. With the team arriving at nine, she hoped she could get what she needed from him quickly. Aleksei Pavlovich described the arsonist as medium-height and medium-build, but looking at the selfies Becky had picked out, Cooper would describe him as more on the scrawny side. She paced the corridor while Tennessee rested his back against the wall and thumbed through photos of his young son on his phone. It gave Cooper an idea.

"You got his file there?" she asked.

He handed it over. "What do you need to know?"

Cooper continued pacing as she read. "Family."

"Easy. Father died last year. Mum's in a home with dementia. Unmarried, but lives with a woman named..." He scrunched up his face as he tried to remember. "Laura Something. Laura has two daughters, the youngest is Kane's."

Cooper closed the file. She hardly needed it after that. "Nice."

An officer emerged from interview suite six and gave them a nod. "He's ready for you. Says he needs a piss, but I reckon he can wait."

Cooper hoped he couldn't. People talked faster when their bladders were full. She and Tennessee entered the room and turned on the recording device.

"Thursday the twentieth of June. Eight twenty-seven p.m. I am DCI Erica Cooper, also present is DS Jack Daniel. Please state your name and date of birth."

He swallowed. "Johnathon Richard Kane, August sixth, erm 1980."

"Pleased to make your acquaintance," Cooper said sarcastically. "Right. I'll make this quick. Our scene of crime officers are top-notch, and our lab is world-class. You can shower, scrub your hands, whatever you like, but if you started those fires, and I believe you did, there will be trace evidence on you. We found your phone at Vixen and location services tracked it to the scene of the other two fires. This isn't looking good for you, is it?"

Kane blinked and mumbled, "No comment."

Tennessee snorted. "You know, you don't actually have to say *no comment*. You can just... not comment."

"Come on DS Daniel," Cooper said. "Give him a break. He left his phone at the scene of a crime; he's not the brightest. Mr Kane, How old is your daughter?"

Kane looked up, he seemed confused. "How did...? She's six."

"Nice age," said Cooper. "Young enough to still worship her father but old enough to feel abandoned when he goes to jail. I wonder what will become of her? A young girl with no father figure around. She might fall in with the wrong crowd, start drinking too young, a bit of weed here, a line of coke there, next thing you know—"

"Don't talk about my girl," he snarled.

She kept her face relaxed, but on the inside, Cooper was smiling. She crossed one leg over the other and decided to push another button. "And your poor mother. She'll never see her pride and joy again."

"Stop it."

Cooper wouldn't stop it. Not yet. She stood up and walked around the desk to get a better view of him. She made a big show of looking him up and down and added, "Don't take this the wrong way Mr Kane, but you're not built for jail. You're too slim to hold your own in a fight, and as for those long eyelashes and full lips, well, I think someone will take a shine to you. Oh, don't look so worried, I'm sure they'll be gentle."

"STOP IT!"

Cooper sat down. "Sentences for arson vary depending on the severity of the damage caused. Considering we're looking at double manslaughter, I think it's safe to say you'll be getting life."

If she didn't have Kane's attention before, she did now. The colour drained from his face as he asked, "Manslaughter? What do you mean, manslaughter?"

Tennessee took this one. "Manslaughter is defined as murder without premeditation."

"I know that." Kane was beginning to flap. He wiped his hand over his mouth, then raked his fingers through his short brown hair. He didn't know where to look. "I mean, I know what manslaughter is, but, b-but why are you talking about manslaughter?"

"Well, Mr Kane, we haven't told the press yet because we're still tracing the families," Tennessee began, "but two office workers died in your little bonfire. That's three counts of arson and two counts of manslaughter. That's life. You'll never see the outside of jail again."

Kane continued to pale. He looked like he could faint at any moment. There was no bravado left in the man, not that there'd been much to start with.

"Laura will visit," Cooper assured him. "She will at first anyway. Then the excuses will begin and she'll miss the odd visit. Then she'll miss two in a row. Then you'll hear on the grapevine that she's seeing someone new; someone who can provide for her girls. Only he's not a good egg. Has a thing for the young ones."

Cooper stopped. She could smell something, and when she looked at Tennessee, the look he gave her meant she hadn't imagined it. Urine. They both slid their chairs back twelve inches.

Tennessee pressed a button. They'd have to pause while Kane got cleaned up.

While they waited for assistance, Cooper leant forward and softened her tone. "Look, Johnny, we both know you didn't wake up this morning and decide to burn down three city-centre bars. Someone told you to do it. Give us the bigger fish, and I'll see what I can do about reducing the charges."

He gawped at his sodden groin. Scared and humiliated. Cooper could see him weighing up his options. What was better, grassing someone in and risking their wrath, or a lifetime behind bars with the nightmares she'd just implanted in his brain?

A big, fat tear rolled down his cheek. She was right; he wouldn't last five minutes in the slammer. Two officers arrived to take Kane to change into a paper boiler suit. When he got to the door, he turned back and met Cooper's gaze. "Hanson," he said. "He's called Wayne Hanson."

Cooper let out the sort of sigh where every last ounce of breath left her lungs. Tennessee slapped her on the back. "Nice work," he said, checking his watch, "and nice timing."

Cooper spoke into the recording device one last time. "Interview terminated eight-fifty p.m."

UNIFORMED OFFICERS AND DETECTIVES alike sat straight-backed despite their stifled yawns and itchy eyes. They were tired. It had been non-stop since the moment Cooper had taken the call about Fletcher Blackburn and Ibrahim Moradi's shooting on Monday evening. Meals had been missed, sleep had been sacrificed, and families had been neglected. It was time to put an end to their suffering.

Keaton was the last to arrive. Her usually neat ponytail was askew but the grin she was wearing told Cooper she'd tracked down the books and had taken them to the lab. She approached Cooper and patted her on the arm. "I waited while Hong ran the prints. Thought you'd want to know straight away."

"And?"

Keaton's face spread into a wide grin. "As suspected."

Relief filled Cooper's heart. She hadn't assembled everyone for no reason. She reached up and cupped Keaton's face in her hands. "You star," she said. "Now do what you do best."

Keaton turned to face rows of her colleagues. "Right, peeps. Switch your phones off and switch your brains on. Court is in session." The room fell silent as eyes turned to Keaton and Cooper. "God gave you two ears, but only one mouth so hush up and listen up."

Cooper had to marvel at the way Keaton commanded her peers. Years of playing and captaining team sports had given the woman a confidence and swagger Cooper could only dream off. Erica Cooper wasn't a wallflower by any stretch of the imagination, but her self-esteem had taken a beating over the last few years between some disastrous relationships and her illness.

Keaton took a seat between Boyd—whom she dwarfed—and Tennessee, who turned to her and whispered, "Decent. A solid eight out of ten. Had to deduct a point for *peeps*."

Cooper had the floor. She perched herself on the edge of a desk and shuffled her weight until she was sat on it. Crossing her legs, she picked up a folder and pulled out her notes. Within half an hour, everyone knew the theory, the evidence that backed it up and what was still conjecture.

"As for Hanson, the phone found at the scene of one of the bar fires led us to Johnathon Kane. He's given up Hanson and will no doubt give us more details once he's dried off and put on some big boy pants. Whyte, Boyd, you two have been tailing Hanson, so it's only right you get the honour of putting him in cuffs. Speak to Kane and arrange some back up for the morning. Grab him at six a.m."

Whyte nodded; Boyd bit her lip.

"I need someone to tail Theo Blackburn," Cooper continued, turning her attention to the back of the room. "I want to know where he spends the night. If he's at Budle Bay, leave him be. Otherwise, drag him out of bed at the crack of dawn."

No one volunteered.

"I'll speak to Nixon about overtime."

Two hands shot up from the back row. *Typical.*

"Thank you," Cooper said to the volunteers. "The rest of us will meet at the outskirts of Budle Bay at five forty-five a.m. Not a second later. We have an early start, so get home and get to bed. Drink some warm milk, or some camomile tea, or screw it, have a wee dram. Whatever works."

She sighed. They'd done it.

"HELLO, STEVEN."

Cooper stepped over the baby herring gull and let out a hearty sigh as she placed a takeaway for three on the kitchen table. Her legs felt heavy, but not as heavy as her eyelids. Tina and Josh emerged, sniffing the air and drooling as they clawed at the paper bags. It was late; they must be famished. Tina grabbed some cutlery, dished out three portions and headed towards the dining table.

"Did you get your homework done?" Cooper asked the teenagers as she sat.

They nodded, mouths already full of spare ribs.

"Finished maths and chemistry," Josh said between bites. "Then, we started watching *Riverdale* on Netflix."

Cooper hadn't heard of it.

"It's a murder mystery!" Tina said.

Josh tore another strip of spare rib meat from the bone. "You only like it because the main character's always taking his shirt off."

Tina kicked Josh under the table. Cooper didn't see it, but she heard him grunt, "Hey! Ouch."

Josh's father picked him at half-ten, and Cooper chose that moment to talk to Tina about her grandfather.

"Listen, T. I have some bad news."

"Is it Dad? Because I've been thinking about it and I don't care what Josh says—"

"It's not your father."

"Good, because I'm not interested—" Tina's eyes suddenly widened, and she made pointed eye contact with Cooper. A rarity. "The cancer's back?"

"No. No, it's not that, T."

Tina collapsed back in her chair. "You scared me."

"Sorry. I didn't mean to scare you, but it's your grandfather. He's really not well. He had a heart attack and needed surgery."

Tina sat very still while she processed that information. "Is he going to die?"

Cooper pinched her nose. She'd tried to push the thought away all day. "No, he's tough as an ox. He'll be fine."

"Are you sure?"

"I hope so."

"Me too. I like Grandad Ben."

"And he likes you. He loves you."

Tina began to tidy the table and prepare Steven's evening meal.

Cooper braced herself because she knew how Tina felt about disruption. "I think we should go and visit him."

Her daughter froze with a syringe full of mashed fish in her hand. "When?"

"As soon as possible."

"Would I be in trouble at school?"

Tina had taken time off school to recover after the events of the last winter. She'd had perfect attendance otherwise. "You won't be in trouble. *I* might be. There'll be a fine to pay but as far as I'm concerned it'll be worth it to have you with me."

Tina scooped Steven up and placed him on her knee. He lifted his beak upwards and began to beg. "How long for?"

"A week. Maybe two. If you need to come home sooner because you miss home or your studying is suffering, we can probably arrange it."

Tina concentrated on Steven for a few moments. "You know me. I can study anywhere."

Cooper got to her feet and kissed Tina on the top of her head. "I was hoping you'd say that. The next flight is Sunday morning. Should I book it?"

Tina nodded. "But we have a problem." She motioned towards the bird on her lap. "A seagull-shaped problem."

The bird would need taking care of. He'd been Tina's project since he fell off the roof as a hatchling and she was determined to give him the care required until he was ready for release.

"We can't ask Dad," Tina said. "He only does nice things if there's something in it for him.

"What about Josh?"

"His Mum's a clean freak."

"Your netball friends?"

Tina shook her head. "No. I don't want them to know how weird I am yet."

"Don't talk like that. You're not weird."

Her daughter stared at her. "Mum, I'm hand-rearing a baby seagull."

Cooper narrowed her eyes. "Okay, you have a point."

"So, what do we do? He can't fledge yet."

She couldn't ask Atkinson. Not when they weren't officially back together yet. She reached over and stroked Steven's feathers. He was unbelievably soft. It would have to be someone from the team. It would be unethical to ask a personal favour of the two newest members, not that she'd ask Whyte anyway, and she didn't know Martin well enough to ask this of him. It had to be Keaton or Tennessee. Keaton would probably make a joke about roasting him with some Maris Piper potatoes, and Tennessee would say yes because he was the sort to always help others and always go the extra mile. It was in his nature. However, Tennessee had an infant at home, a wife struggling with parenthood and an elderly mother-in-law. They could do without a creature that, if you weren't careful, would give you a nasty bout of salmonella.

Cooper sighed. "I'll ask Paula."

- Chapter 27 -

Half four and the first blush of pink was creeping over Tynemouth's horizon. A hint of blue sky penetrated the darkness before the pink gave way to burnt orange and stained wispy stratus clouds with rose gold. Moments later, the sun burst free, dissipating the thinnest clouds into nothing. Cooper drained her coffee and headed for the door, her mind torn between Northumberland and the Canaries. Upstairs, a restless Tina had given up on sleep and had instead begun typing a list of caregiving instructions for Steven. In a nearby suburb, Hayley Daniel clutched her baby to her chest as she watched her husband leave for work. A familiar dread crawled into her stomach, as it had done every time he left since Alfie was born. Twenty miles south, Eddie Blackburn clenched and relaxed his fists over and over. It had started to sink in that his little brother would not be visiting him this month, or next month, or ever again. His anger had been like a thick fog that he was unable to navigate through. But over last night's dinner, depression had started to nibble away at the anger, started to dull it. He had to be careful. Depression couldn't regain an empire, but anger could. Sixty-five miles north, Eddie's niece and nephews lay awake, staring at their respective ceilings. His son slept soundly.

A LONE LIGHT WAS on at the Blackburns' barn conversation in Budle Bay. As Cooper and her colleagues approached, Charlene Blackburn could be seen hunched over their large kitchen island, a cup of something hot clutched in her hands. They tiptoed up the gravelled driveway before knocking gently. Charlene jumped and clutched her chest. It took a moment for her to relax and come to answer the door.

"Is everything okay?" she asked nervously.

Cooper was keen to bring this whole dreadful business to a close. "Could you wake the others, please? I'd like everyone in the kitchen."

Charlene glanced from Cooper to Tennessee, then to Keaton and Martin. Her eyes caught sight of another officer waiting in the driveway. She wouldn't know about the vehicles stationed at either end of the B1342: one in Bamburgh, and one at Waren Mill. No one was jumping in their flashy car and making a run for it. Fletcher's second wife nodded silently and padded from the hallway towards the stairwell.

Ten minutes later and three of the Blackburns, still in their nightwear, gathered around the large kitchen island. Charlene tightened her silk robe and sipped fresh coffee. To her left, George cleaned his glasses on plaid print pyjamas and Dylan, in grey camouflage shorts, folded his arms over his bare chest. The kitchen was fitted with spotlighting that accentuated Dylan's indented skull and cast his eyes in shadow. "This had better be good," he grumbled, checking his watch.

"Where's your sister?" Tennessee asked.

Dylan snorted. "The princess is still in bed."

"And your cousin?"

Dylan's look darkened. "In the princess's chamber," he growled.

"Are my ears burning?" Theo Blackburn pushed open a heavy oak door and joined the group in the kitchen. Baggy joggers trailed on the floor, his bare chest bore red fingernail scratches and his hair was loose with dark waves skimming his collar bones. He typed on a mobile as he walked. "Lily's in the shower. She said there'd better be coffee on the go. So what's so important we had to—" He looked up, his eyes narrowing upon Cooper. "Ah fuck, what do you want at this hour? You know, if my father was here we'd be given the fucking respect of a lie-in."

Cooper cut him off. "If your father were here, you'd be the one in jail. We all know he took the fall for your freedom." She stopped, briefly thinking of her own father. Thank goodness she'd be with him soon. She and Tina would go straight from baggage claim to the hospital and shower Ben in affection. Cooper pushed the thought aside and returned to Theo. "You'd be serving time for arson, you little pyromaniac, manslaughter too. So I suggest you stop whinging. Now, as for why I wanted you all here, I thought you'd like to know who killed your uncle."

Theo stopped, put his phone in the back pocket of his joggers and smirked at Dylan. The big man met his gaze with daring intensity, challenging him to say something. Anything.

Tennessee positioned himself between the Blackburns and their kitchen door. "In respect to the attempted murder of Fletcher Blackburn—"

"Whoa. Hang on a minute." Theo addressed the elephant in the room. "What do you mean *attempted*?" He made air quotes with his fingers. "My uncle is dead and rotting in the morgue. I mean, I didn't *see* the body, but—"

"*I* saw the body," Charlene snapped. Her eyes were filling with tears, and she looked like she could throw her scalding coffee over him. "I saw the body of my husband. The man I loved. He was shot. Show him some damn respect."

Theo gave her a condescending smile before opening the fridge. "What? No beer?"

Charlene stood up, unable to stay still any longer. "My husband was shot, DS Daniel. Twice. There was no attempted murder. He was murdered."

"Actually, Mrs Blackburn," Tennessee began, "before he was shot, Fletcher was poisoned. His autopsy showed high levels of digoxin, a poison derived from foxgloves."

The Blackburns looked at each other, perhaps visualising the impressive gardens at Morshaw Manor, its flowerbeds adorned with white and purple foxgloves amongst snapdragons and peonies.

Keaton stepped forward, she placed a file on the kitchen island and removed some images from it. "On Thursday the sixth of June, two books were checked out of Wooler library: Death In The Garden and Plants That Kill." She pointed to pictures of the two books. "They were checked out using your library card, Theo."

All eyes turned to Theo Blackburn, who froze for a moment then raised his hands. "No. No way. Don't bloody drag me into this. I don't even have a fucking library card."

"Oh, but you do." Keaton tweaked her ponytail. "It was applied for online using your name and details. Don't take this the wrong way, Theo, but I take you to be the sort of man who'd use the word *password* as his password, or maybe *one, two, three, four*. Whoever applied for this library card must have been in a hurry because they didn't choose a password that any average Joe would pick. They chose something that only they would know and that they'd easily remember. It was, all-one-word, *angel wings and butterflies*."

George jumped from his seat. "Shit."

The room erupted. George resembled a cornered animal, wide-eyed and looking for a way out. Charlene was the first to speak, crying out a pained "No!" She reached out and firmly grabbed his arm. "George? No. I— I don't believe it."

"Believe it," said Keaton. "Funny you used the word *shit* there, George. Because that's exactly how I'd describe your poetry, of course, I'm not your target audience. I like dance music, anything fast that I can workout too. The chief here, she likes rock music and a bit of metal. This handsome fella is a cheesy pop kind of guy, but he'll deny it—"

"Focus, Paula," Cooper said with a smirk while Tennessee grumbled something about cheese.

"*Angel wings and butterflies* is a line from a poem you wrote," Keaton continued. "A poem we believe is about Charlene."

Charlene immediately let go of George's arm. "What?"

George turned away, unable to look at her.

"Your Oedipus complex is none of my business, but the evidence is." Keaton pointed to the pictures of the books from Wooler library. "Your prints are on the covers of both books, and I'm willing to bet my house that your prints are all over pages seventy-five to seventy-eight in Plants That Kill and page thirty-three of Death In The Garden. Those are the pages that detail foxgloves."

Cooper leant forward. "Your father had a health shake every morning, didn't he?"

George nodded.

Placing another photo on the island, Cooper continued. "The foxgloves at Morshaw were pruned recently, as shown here and here. You took the leaves and stems and blended them with kale and spinach after your step-mother used the blender on Monday morning."

He swallowed but said nothing.

"You should have cleaned it more thoroughly because the lab found digoxin on the blades. The family meeting began, and you handed your father his death smoothie."

"You bastard," Charlene cried. She ran at George, pumping her fists into his chest over and over. George didn't fight back or even try to defend himself. Theo did nothing to stop her. He seemed to find some sick humour in his cousin trying to frame him for murder. Keaton gently wrapped her arms around Charlene and guided her back to a seat.

"I don't regret it," George said. "He deserved it. Everyone will be happier now he's gone." His chest heaved. He extended his arms, palms up, and awaited the cuffs. Keaton, who was nearest, obliged. "You'll be happier," he said, turning to Charlene. "You will. Trust me. I tried to warn you about him, but you didn't listen. I could see it in his eyes. He was starting to look at you the way he used to look at Mum. Like you were, I don't know, some sort of pet. A pretty little creature that he could crush the second he got tired of it, or the second it dared to disobey him. He would have gone on to abuse you like he abused everyone else. I couldn't let that happen, though. And you're young enough to escape all this. I saw his will in the office. You'll be set. You don't have to be a part of any of this. You're free now."

Charlene's face was set like stone. "I didn't want to be free," she said, barely moving her lips. "I didn't need saving, and you had no right... no right to play God like that."

George's glasses slipped down his nose. He nudged his face against his shoulder to try and push them back up. "I tried a few times. A petal here, a petal there. I was trying to use as little as possible, and I knew it was working because his eyes had started to turn yellow over the last few days and he'd stopped eating. I used a little extra on Monday, added some leaves and stems, then I put the smoothie on Dad's desk, but Dylan said he was thirsty and took a sip. I tried to stop him." He blinked slowly, as if his eyelids were suddenly heavier.

"Hang on," Dylan rubbed his temples. "Is that why my head was killing me all day?"

Cooper nodded. "I think so. You injuries mean you're more susceptible to headaches. The poison affected you very quickly. A few sips wouldn't be enough to kill you, but it was enough to make you very ill."

Dylan moved towards George, but nothing about his demeanour seemed angry. He hugged his little brother, and that's when Cooper scrutinised his expression. It was pride. Admiration almost.

George allowed Keaton to peel him away from Dylan and take him by the arm. She guided him through the door to the courtyard where officers waited to escort him to HQ.

Dylan called after him. "I didn't think you had it in you."

George's face cracked. "No one ever did."

THE DOBERMANN WENT BERSERK at the sound of Elliot Whyte pressing Hanson's doorbell. It was quarter to six in the morning, and the only other sign of life in Rowlands Gill was a baker delivering goodies to the café across the road. He paused to take a gander at Whyte and Boyd as they stood on Hanson's doorstep but scarpered as soon as the door began to creak open.

Hanson's voice could be heard from behind the door. "Gazza! Bugger off will you."

The Dobermann was possessed. Barking and clawing to get to the intruders. Boyd took a step backwards and looked to Whyte for support. She always looked so vulnerable with those big eyes and something about her appearance made him think of a deer or a bunny from a Disney film. She was capable though, she proved that by finding the chef, interviewing him, following up on his alibi and eliminating him from the investigation. She had a good head on her shoulders. Twice he'd tried to subtly ask if she was single—twice he'd bottled it. He didn't want a repeat of the Cooper incident. That was going to haunt him till the day he retired. Best stick to civilian women. Besides, Martin clearly had a thing for Boyd. The atmosphere may always be strained between him and Cooper, but he didn't need to add to it by becoming anyone's love rival. Whyte flashed Boyd a reassuring smile and clutched his retractable baton. He gestured to one of their back up units to keep their distance, then signalled to another to move around the back of the property.

Eventually, the barking subsided. It sounded as if the Dobermann was being dragged to another room and given a stern, "Stay!"

Hanson appeared in his dressing gown. "Fucking hell," he moaned when he saw the panda cars. "Bring the whole squadron, did you? What in God's name do you want? I already spoke to that Martin fella and the hefty woman." His brows quickly lowered. "Wait. I know you. You were at the hospital," he said, pointing at Boyd. "On the children's ward. And you," his finger moved to Whyte, "you were at the Shell garage... and Tesco." It dawned on him. "You fuckers have been tailing me."

"Glad you could catch up," Whyte said dryly.

"What's this all about?" He checked his watch. "I have a sick daughter who I'm supposed to be having breakfast with at seven."

"The only person you'll be having breakfast with is Harrison Pace."

"And who the bloody hell is he?"

Whyte and Boyd's back up moved to either side of them. Four against one—if you didn't count the massive dog.

"He's a known troublemaker who my colleagues picked up last night on drug-related offences. He'll be your cellmate when we return to the station. Big guy by all accounts and I hear he has a thing for French maids."

Boyd tried to suppress a laugh, but it escaped as a snort and she quickly looked away from Hanson who's face had turned beetroot with rage. His posture changed to one of aggression: chest inflated, shoulder's rounded, jaw clenched. It was his eyes that gave him away: they flickered with fear.

"What do you mean *cellmate*? I didn't touch Fletcher. Didn't lay a finger on him. I have an alibi, don't I? I swear you're making a big mistake, lad."

If Whyte didn't approve of being called *lad*, he didn't show it. "I'm not making a mistake, and I know you didn't kill Fletcher."

Hanson was incandescent, his voice loud enough to wake the neighbours. "Then why the fuck are you wasting my time?"

Whyte didn't answer straight away. He was enjoying watching him squirm. "On Wednesday evening, you received a phone call that made you very angry. We know what number that call came from."

Boyd rattled off the number. "That number is registered to a little old lady who lives in Berwick."

"I don't know any little old ladies from Berwick," snarled Hanson.

"I believe you," Whyte said. "She reported her phone as stolen back in May. Some arsehole mugged her on her way back from doing her weekly shop. The wise guy who's been using said phone—and I use the term *wise guy* in an ironic sense—forgot to fully disable location services. Yesterday morning, that phone was on Westgate

Road at eight minutes past eleven, the Cloth Market at twenty-seven minutes past eleven and Stepney Lane at twelve-oh-one. Do those locations mean anything to you?"

Hanson glowered. "Should they?"

"Stop bullshitting me. Two people died. They're the locations of McDermott's, The Silver Mirror and Vixen."

"That doesn't prove anything."

"No" Whyte conceded. "But the testimony of the man who was using that phone does. My colleagues picked him up in the Tanners Arms last night and he's singing like a karaoke-lovin' canary. McDermott's, The Silver Mirror and Vixen have been paying the Blackburns for aeons. I believe you ordered the fires as payback for the murders of your associates in Frankland. You wanted to hit them in their wallets, where you knew it would really hurt."

Hanson looked back over his shoulder. Whyte didn't know if he was considering making a bolt for the back door or if he was about to release Gazza.

"Don't even think about it," Whyte urged, covering both bases. "Mr Hanson, I am arresting you for arson and manslaughter."

The two back up officers moved in and wrestled a struggling Hanson into handcuffs while Whyte finished reading Hanson his rights.

As he was led away to an awaiting patrol car, Whyte turned to Boyd. "You want to give him the good news?"

She brightened and opened her mouth but quickly changed her mind, fear getting the better of her. "I'll let you," she told Whyte.

Whyte would spend time later wondering why she was so skittish, but for now, he relished passing on some information to Wayne Hanson.

"Mr Hanson, a lovely lady from the National Crime Agency can't wait to meet you. She took an overnight train and will be at the station in time for your arrival."

As well as the NCA, a team from the North East Regional Special Operations Unit—who went by the rather rubbish acronym NERSOU—would also be waiting. Still, they weren't the only ones who wanted a piece of Hanson. News vans from the BBC, ITV, Sky and Channel Four would be clamouring for the best view of the front of HQ. Someone bearing an uncanny resemblance to Saffron Boyd had tipped them off.

- Chapter 28 -

George grinned as he was led away. Cooper had seen her fair share of Cheshire Cats in cuffs. Some smiled in bravado, a way of covering their fear of jail and what awaited them. Others gave evil smirks, trying to force fear upon the arresting officer. "Wait until I get out. I'll have some fun with you," one predatory man told Cooper back when she was new to the force and Whyte had left her alone with a suspected rapist to chase down his accomplice. And some smiled because, frankly, they were off their rockers. George's smile was new to Cooper and she strongly suspected it was a smile of relief. He'd done what he had to do to protect Charlene and his family, and now they were free of their overbearing father, and he was free of the secret he'd been carrying. Nothing about jail could scare him as much as his father had.

Once the car pulled away and the sound of its engine faded to nothing, Cooper pulled her attention back to the remaining Blackburns. There were looks of shock on all their faces.

"I don't believe it." Charlene was holding a folded tea towel over her face and breathing through it as a way to stop herself from hyperventilating.

"The scrawny geek's got some balls on him," Theo said. "But that was attempted murder. You said so yourself," he turned to Cooper. "George didn't shoot anyone. His balls aren't that big. He hated guns. Almost pissed himself when I took him on a pheasant shoot when we were teenagers."

Cooper pulled her lips in and looked to the floor. Part of her didn't want to do this, but a more significant part knew it was her job and the right thing to do. "You're right. George didn't shoot Fletcher." She looked up. "I think it's time we got Lily out of the shower."

Theo froze, his mouth slightly ajar and his eyes narrowed to slits. "What? You're joking?" He shook his head.

"I'm sorry. I'm not." Cooper asked Tennessee and Martin to wait with the others while she and Keaton, as the female detectives, followed the sound of running water.

The stairwell was a mix of modern and old. The original stone steps were adorned with a handrail made of chrome and glass. The walls were decorated with Georgia O'Keefe prints in black frames with thick white mounts. All lilies, Cooper noted.

"Lily?" Cooper knocked on a bedroom door. "Lily, it's DCI Cooper. I'm coming in with DS Keaton." Lily's room at Budle Bay was markedly different from her room at Morshaw. At Morshaw the room was fit for a princess. Girlie. This room was more for a queen; it was tasteful and grown-up. The room was neutral with accents of teal. It featured a king-sized bed with a padded headboard, its sheets still crumpled from last night's activities. A velveteen chaise longue was pointed towards a window with a sea view, and an antique dresser sat flush against the opposite wall.

"Nice," Keaton muttered.

"Lily?" Cooper called again. She stood at the door to the en suite. It was ajar and swirls of steamy air were pouring through the gap. She glanced through the opening. The glass surround of a large shower cubicle was speckled with water droplets, but beyond the glass, as steamy as it was, there was no movement.

"Shit." Cooper burst into the en suite, knocking over a bottle of perfume and tripping on a pile of clothes. The perfume bottle shattered, sending its over-powering fruity scents into the air. Cooper raced to the window where two words were scrawled onto the pane in rose-coloured lipstick: *I'm sorry*.

"She's gone," Cooper growled. She lowered the toilet lid and climbed up, using it as a step. Pushing open the window as wide as she could, she scanned the surrounding country lanes, fields of sheep and grass-covered dunes. "LILY!" she yelled, but there was no sign of the youngest Blackburn.

In the bedroom, Keaton pulled her handheld radio from her belt and quickly dispatched instructions to the units in the area. She looked out the bedroom window, angling her head to the courtyard. "The cars are still there."

"She went on foot," Cooper said as she jumped off the toilet lid and raced toward the stairs, skidding in the pool of perfume and gagging as the fragrance found its way into her mouth and eyes. "There's a tree branch under the window. Easily thick enough to take her weight." When she reached the kitchen, Theo was her first target. "Where is she?"

"What?" Theo looked taken aback.

"Lily. Where did Lily go? Tell me now or—"

Cooper didn't get to finish her threat.

"What do you mean, *where is she?* She's upstairs." He pointed to the ceiling.

"No, she's not."

Theo ran towards the stairs to check for himself. Satisfied that the upstairs of the house was empty, he returned and made for the front door.

"Not so fast," Cooper warned. "Stay here with DS Daniel. Jack, find out what he knows. Martin, you're with me."

"I— I don't know anything. First, you tell me Lily killed Uncle Fletcher. Now you're saying she's run off and I that know where—"

Cooper ignored Theo and scrambled to the courtyard where a handful of officers awaited her. Dylan Blackburn followed, pulling a pair of grubby trainers onto bare feet and sliding his thick arms into the sleeves of a knitted jumper.

"Stay with your cousin, Dylan."

"Not a chance." He locked eyes with Cooper, and she knew in an instant he wouldn't be persuaded without the use of force, and she would need a truckload of force to restrain a man like Dylan Blackburn. "My Mum's gone, my dad's dead, brother's going to jail. I need to hear from Lily what happened."

She nodded—like he would take any other answer—and called for Keaton. "Paula, the units in Waren Mill and Bamburgh?"

"Roadblocks are ready. They have Lily's description and will radio if they see anyone who even remotely looks like her. There are local units on their way to provide assistance as well. I've sent a photo of Lily to their sarge."

"Good. Have them check the caravan sites and campgrounds. Right, she's probably avoiding the main road. Paula, Martin, take four men and head inland. The rest of you, Dylan, we'll follow the coastal route. Leave no stone unturned."

Keaton instantly took charge of her team. They took off at a quick pace and split into pairs to cover the trails that Keaton pointed out.

"Dylan, are there any outhouses on the property? Sheds? Somewhere Lily could hide?"

He scanned about. "Yeah, there's a shed in the back garden and an old den we made when we were younger."

Cooper pointed to one of the uniforms. "Go check them out."

The rest of them headed down a country lane towards the sea. They peered over stone walls and squinted into dense bushes. Cooper constantly surveyed the horizon, her eyes programmed to pick up the first hint of movement. Not wanting to spook Lily, she moved quietly and refrained from calling her name. "How's your relationship with Lily?" she asked Dylan as they reached the edge of the dunes.

"I call her a spoiled brat; she calls me a dickhead. But," he paused, looking about, "I try to look out for her, and she doesn't talk to me like I'm a fucking idiot."

"Is she scared of you?"

He shook his head. "No. She might be the only God-damned person in the world who sees past what I look like."

Cooper's eyes started to sting. She blinked back a tear. Now was not the time to feel sorry for a criminal, even though that was precisely how she was feeling. "Call for her," she whispered. "She might show herself for you."

Dylan moved through the dunes calling Lily's name. Not too loud, not too urgent. His heavy feet sank into the sand as he walked and even Cooper, who was considerably lighter, felt her legs being sapped of energy with each step that she took in the loose sand. When they reached the beach, Dylan turned to her. "North or south?"

Picturing a map of the area in her mind, Cooper tried to place herself in Lily's shoes. "The tide's in. If she went north, she'd either have to cross the estuary or stick to the roads. Either way, the unit at Waren Mill will spot her. I say we head south. Keep covering the dunes and move towards the holiday cottages, she could be sheltering there."

They turned south, spreading out to cover as much ground as they could. "Tucker?" she called to a uniform. "Head down to the beach. Check any caves. There's a couple of boats down there too. Give them a once over."

"Ma'am," he replied, turning away and heading to the shore.

The worn path had shrubs to one side and dunes to the other, but even the heady scent of salty air mixed with heather couldn't cover the perfume seeping through Cooper's clothing. It made her feel sick. She pulled her jacket off, discarded it on a rock and shivered, for although the sun was up, it had yet to warm the sea breeze. Dylan continued to call for his sister, leaving long gaps between calls so they could listen for a reply or the sound of footsteps. Tucker neared a stone pier that jutted out into the estuary and looked up the steep bank to Cooper. She pointed towards the pier, wanting him to check both sides as well as the pieces of rock that had crumbled away.

Where was she? The only signs of life were the seagulls above and the wading birds below. Cooper withdrew her radio and touched base with Keaton. "Any luck?"

"Nothing yet, boss."

Ahead, a flat area of concrete was partially consumed by green ferns and nettles. It looked out of place amongst the unrelenting natural coastline that surrounded it. As Cooper approached, it dawned on her that it wasn't simply a flat piece of concrete: it was a roof. A structure was built into the dunes with small, circular openings drilled into otherwise solid grey walls. She'd found the World War II gun encampment. Cooper and Dylan exchanged a look, nodded to each other and approached the entrance. The building was small, only a few metres across, and it was slowly being reclaimed by nature. Patches of grey concrete were turning green from microscopic plant life.

"Lily?" Dylan whispered. "Lily, are you in there?"

They entered the dark space. The only light came from a panoramic hole that framed a perfect view of the estuary and its pristine white sand. In the distance, Holy Island towered out of the waves of the North Sea. A circle of round metal pegs poked out of a mounting plate where an enormous gun would have once sat, protecting the northeast from invading forces. Cooper turned around in the gloomy room. Under a solid concrete shelf, a shivering Lily Blackburn crouched, holding a broken bottle to her neck.

- Chapter 29 -

The sharp edge of the bottle pressed into Lily's pale flesh. It hadn't cut through a major vein or artery, but it had pierced the skin. A rivulet of scarlet blood ran down her neck and chest. Her face was deathly white, except for some yellowing under one eye and on her jaw. Her pupils were twice the size they'd normally be. The youngest Blackburn shivered, wearing only a thin set of silky pyjamas and white socks that were now soaked through and stained with mud and grass. Cooper spied further cuts and grazes on her shins and forearms.

"Stay back," Lily blurted, pressing the glass firmly into her neck, causing the blood to flow quicker.

"It's okay, Lily." Cooper spoke calmly and took a step back to avoid crowding the frightened girl. "You look cold. I can get you a blanket."

Lily shook her head and sniffed, "I want Theo."

Not wanting Lily to harm herself further, or end up taking her own life, Cooper radioed for Tennessee and asked him to bring Theo as quickly as he could. "Arrange an ambulance," she added quietly. "No sirens."

"Is he coming?"

"He's on his way," Cooper assured her. "Please, Lily. You're freezing. Do you want your brother's jumper?"

Lily's eyes darted back and forth between Cooper and Dylan. Eventually, she nodded. "But stay there," she warned him.

Dylan stayed where he was, removed his jumper and tossed it onto the floor a foot or so from where Lily sat. She pulled it towards her using her foot. "I don't want to go to jail. I can't."

"Your family will do everything they can to stop that happening, Lily." Cooper kept her distance but crouched down so she could be eye-level with Lily.

Dylan nodded. "Of course. Whatever happened, we'll fix it."

The Blackburns had good lawyers. They needed to with the sort of things Eddie and Fletcher had got up to over the years.

"And if I'm right about what I think happened," Cooper continued, "I'll try my best to help you as well."

Lily looked surprised.

"I'm serious. I'm not here to frame you or paint you in a bad light. I promise you that. I only want the truth. I'll be fair, and importantly, so will the judge."

The bottle moved ever so slightly. There was a noise at the entrance to the bunker before Theo edged his way in. For someone who was usually so cocksure and arrogant, he looked nervous.

"What happened, babe? Jesus, you're bleeding."

He moved forward, saw her shaking arm holding the bottle to her neck and froze. He raised his hands and stepped back.

Dylan wrapped his arms around himself. "You wanted Theo. He's here now. So how about you put the bottle down and he can give you a hug and then we can get you somewhere warmer."

Lily wavered, but the glass remained pressed into her skin.

Cooper looked up at Theo and Dylan. From her crouched position, they looked even bigger than usual. "She needs medical attention, but we can't do anything while she has a weapon. I can't risk her hurting herself."

Theo looked like he wanted to say something but couldn't find the right words. Dylan took a deep breath. "Come on, Lil. Put the bottle down. You heard the detective; she wants to help you."

"That's right," Cooper said. "I'm not going to rush over and arrest you." She looked back to Theo. "Has the ambulance arrived?"

He nodded.

"Could you ask for some blankets?"

Theo left. Cooper was freezing, Lily more so, and now Dylan had given up his jumper, Cooper suspected he was also suffering from the cold of the morning. When Theo returned, he was carrying a pile of green fleece blankets. Cooper reached up and took two. One for herself and one for Lily. "Here, put this round you."

Cooper shuffled a little closer to Lily and tilted her head at Dylan. Slowly, he joined them and sat himself down next to his sister. He opened his hand and she slipped her free hand into his. It looked so tiny, almost doll-like, in Dylan's shovel-sized palm. He closed his fingers around hers and squeezed gently.

"No one's going to rush you, Lily," Cooper told her. "No one is going to grab you or try to wrestle the bottle from you. I don't want you or your brother to get hurt, okay?"

Lily blinked but said nothing. Tears began to stream from her eyes; a translucent version of the red that flowed down her neck.

"Right, I'm going to start at the beginning, and I want you to stop me if I go wrong." Cooper swallowed nervously. "You had a very sheltered upbringing. You couldn't date who you wanted to," her eyes flicked to Theo, "you couldn't work where you wanted to. You were expected to cook and clean and take care of the men in your family. But that wasn't the life you wanted. You wanted...fame? Fortune?"

"No," Lily said with a sniffle, lifting her eyes from the grubby floor of the bunker. "I didn't want to be a celebrity or anything. Not really. I just wanted... more."

"But nice clothes and likes on social media made you feel good? They validated you."

She nodded. "I guess." Further tears snaked down her flushed cheeks.

"That's nothing to be ashamed of. It's normal. But a part-time job at a beautician's didn't pay for the labels you like to wear. I know you call yourself an influencer, and I might be older and more out of the loop than people your age, but I'm no dinosaur either. I had a look at your account; you have less than a thousand followers. I doubt anyone is gifting sunglasses worth over eight hundred pounds to an account with those numbers. You bought those glasses yourself, didn't you?"

Lily wiped her face on the back of her hand, wincing as she touched yellow flesh near her eye. "Yes."

Cooper was glad Lily was talking, and she seemed to be warming up slightly. Her shivering was less pronounced. "You didn't really know what your father did for a living, did you?"

She shook her head.

"But you knew what Charlene used to do. She didn't hide it. You knew she earned great money, and you wanted some of that, so, you took a job at Vixen."

"YOU WHAT?" Theo's attitude changed in an instant from that of a concerned boyfriend to an angry abuser. "You danced for dirty old men?" he spat, stepping forward to tower over the weeping Lily.

Lily flinched, cowering further into the corner. "I— I just danced. I didn't strip or anything, Theo."

"Back off," Dylan warned, his teeth bared at his cousin.

Theo ignored him. "You little slapper."

Rage coursed through Cooper. The word stung her as much as it stung Lily. "Out," she commanded, pushing Theo in the chest. He didn't budge. She saw Tennessee and Tucker lurking in the shadows, ready to assist if needed. "Do I need to remind you, Theo, that I can reopen the Harbour Lights case any time I damn well like? Now get out." He looked at her as if she wouldn't dare and when she raised her right brow to challenge him, he ground his jaw, folded his arms and walked away.

Cooper let out a sigh and realised her hands were shaking. She wiggled her fingers for a few moments while she calmed down before continuing to talk to Lily. "The money was good at Vixen. You worked the quiet afternoon shifts as it meant you could juggle it with your job at the beautician's, and you always made it home for dinner. No one would be suspicious. No one would know. You had no idea your family charged protection fees to the owner."

Cooper faced Dylan, who was massaging his temples. His hands were so large he could rub both sides of his head with one hand. "Dylan, the owner of Vixen—Aleksei Pavlovich—told me you never go in the bar."

"Yeah. I... I make the girls nervous. I can see it in their faces. They don't like to look at me."

Cooper felt for him. He was a brute all right, but he was also the product of his upbringing. She'd been sneered at when she pushed a pram while wearing her school uniform, and kids had pointed when the wig she used to wear would slip. But she'd never know what it was like to be Dylan, to wear the damage of abuse so obviously.

"Aleksei said you'd go to the back door and wait for one of the bartenders to bring out the cash. Then you'd take off."

"Yeah. I didn't like to hang around."

"But you were ill on Monday. Poisoned. So Fletcher did the rounds himself. He wasn't going to let the fact he was nauseous and probably seeing double come between him and his money."

"Not when he'd already called me every name under the sun for taking a sick day."

"Do you think your father was the sort to just go to the back door of a gentleman's club?"

He shorted, but not out of amusement. "Not a chance. There's no way he'd go to Vixen or Bambi Bar, or any of those clubs, and not go in to take a look at the girls."

Cooper carefully leaned forward and patted Lily on her knee. "Aleksei said your father's mood suddenly changed. He described your father as happy but sickly-looking one minute, then like he was ready to kill someone the next. He saw you, didn't he?"

Lily's mouth opened, and she gasped for breath, her eyes pleading with the ceiling as if asking for forgiveness. It took several minutes and a lot of soothing words from her brother before she was able to speak through the panic.

"I came out of the dressing room and got on the stage. He was sat there, drinking whiskey and... and... our eyes met. I panicked. I didn't know what to do. He stormed out of there so fast. I just jumped off the stage and ran back to the dressing room. I couldn't go back on after that. I couldn't do anything."

"Where did he wait for you?" Cooper asked.

"The back alley." She doubled up. Her shoulders rounded, head bowed, legs crossed in front of her. She looked half the size she was; like someone who wanted to be so small that they'd disappear. "I put my jacket on. I wanted some fresh air because it was like I couldn't breathe. I grabbed a packet of cigarettes and went out the back to have a smoke, but my hands were shaking so much I couldn't light it. His... his car came screeching round the corner. He got out and dragged me into it."

Dylan formed his free hand into a fist and cracked his knuckles.

"He raced home. Speeding. I was sure we were going crash into a tree and go up in flames. I was crying, and he was calling me all sorts. I told him that he never called Charlene those names, but it made him even madder. He said it was different, that I was his daughter and I was an embarrassment. He grabbed me by my hair and dragged me into the house."

Terror gripped Lily, she squeezed her eyes shut, grabbing Dylan's hand so tightly the ends of his fingers turned pink. Her other arm slammed downward, shattering the bottle against the concrete floor. Shards of green glass ricocheted off the wall next to her; the bottleneck, with its knife-like edges, remained clasped in Lily's hand.

"Take your time," Cooper said as calmly as she could. "There's no rush."

"I kept asking Mo to help me. I begged him."

"But he'd never go against his employer?"

She shook her head from side to side. "It was like he couldn't even hear me. Dad— Dad dragged me into his office and slammed the door. He was slapping me, punching me." She took her hand away from Dylan's and touched the tender skin around her eye. "I fell to the floor and curled up. I wrapped my hands around my head to protect myself... but he started kicking me instead."

Dylan winced. The story of abuse all too familiar to the eldest of Fletcher's children.

"He wouldn't stop. He just kept kicking me, over and over. I tried to crawl under the desk to get away from him... and I saw the gun, taped under there... I thought... I thought he was going to kill me."

"I believe you," Cooper said. "You grabbed the gun. Then what?"

"He backed away for a second, long enough for me to clamber to my feet and move towards the door. I wanted to make a run for it. I was going to pack a bag and go to Theo's." She grimaced, perhaps recalling how Theo had just spoken to her. "Then Dad lunged at me and the gun went off. I... I don't remember pulling the trigger. He fell over the desk and onto the floor. Then I shot him again. That time, well, I suppose that wasn't an accident. I had to make sure he didn't get back up. I killed him. Oh, God. I killed Dad." She screamed, pulling her blanket open and stabbing the bottleneck into her thigh, once, twice—

Dylan lunged, grasping her hand in his. "Stop, Lily. I won't let you do this."

He pulled the make-shift weapon free and tossed it from the bunker's window. Cooper heard it shatter. Dylan quickly folded a blanket and pressed it to Lily's leg, stemming the flow of blood, but only for a moment; a circle of red was already blooming on the green fabric.

"It's okay, Lily. It's okay."

"Time to get her out of here," Cooper said. She motioned for Tennessee to get a paramedic, but Dylan had already scooped her up and was carrying her towards the exit. The three of them blinked as they emerged into the sunlight. Two paramedics helped Dylan lay Lily on a stretcher in the back of the ambulance. The shorter of the two cleaned her wounds while the other secured her to the bed ready for transport."

"Berwick?" The shorter one asked, referring to the nearest big town.

The taller one shook his head and tightened a strap around Lily's legs. "Too much blood loss. We'll take her to Cramlington. We need to floor it."

"Dylan," Cooper called. "Go with DS Daniel; he'll follow the ambulance. I don't have time to argue. We need to go now."

Thankfully, he did as he was asked and jumped from the vehicle. Tennessee already had the door to a squad car open and ready for him. As the doors shut, Cooper asked how she could help.

"Hold this."

Cooper pressed clean gauze against Lily's neck. She looked even paler.

"I didn't want to shoot Mo," she said, her breathing shallow but rapid. "I was frightened, and I knew he was armed. I thought he'd shoot me if he saw me with the gun, so I just... You know."

Stroking her hair, Cooper tried to relax Lily as the ambulance raced south along the A1. When they arrived at the Specialist Emergency Care Hospital, they were met by a team of surgeons and nurses who wheeled Lily away through double doors. It was four and a half hours before Cooper saw her again.

Cooper didn't think Lily was a danger to the public, but following protocol, she had to arrange for officers to monitor the ward at all times. Regardless of Lily's reasons, she'd still need to be taken into custody for the time being, and Cooper couldn't risk her doing another runner.

Greeting a pair of officers, Cooper and Tennessee briefly spoke with Lily's surgeon before following him onto the ward. There were only two patients in the eight-bed ward, and they had been placed in opposite corners of the long room. The doctor pulled back a curtain and busied himself with charts, heart rates and blood pressure readings. Next to the bed, Dylan snored loudly in an uncomfortable-looking chair.

Cooper smiled at Lily. "How are you feeling?"

"She'll be woozy for a while," answered the doctor on Lily's behalf. "And Lily, you didn't react too well to the anaesthetic. If you continue feeling nauseous, just press this button."

She blinked wearily but brightened when she saw Dylan next to her.

"You'll have to go over all of this again later, but I hoped you could clear a few things up for us," Cooper said.

She lowered her eyes, then nodded once.

"What were you wearing when your father dragged you back to Morshaw?"

"Erm... a bikini, a red one, with a denim jacket and heels."

"These heels?" Cooper showed her a photo that had been taken of the inside of Lily's wardrobe.

Another nod.

"We had an expert bloodstain analyst assess your father's study. I released Charlene and initially dismissed you as a suspect because our expert told me the shooter had to be between five-foot-ten and six-foot-two. How tall are you?"

"I'm five-five."

"Even in a pair of high heels, you'd still only be five-eight, five-nine at a push. But these..." she tapped on a pair of shoes with see-through heels that had caught her eye during the search for handwriting samples. "These are eight-inch perspex platform heels. Otherwise known as..."

"Stripper heels," Lily answered with a sigh.

"Which means, on Monday, you were six-foot-one."

Dylan stirred. "Hey, you're awake," he said with a smile. It was the first time Cooper had seen him look happy.

Something was troubling Cooper. She asked, "Why did you write Hanson's name in your father's diary?"

"I didn't know who he was at first, but I kept hearing his name around the house—the Hanson meeting this and the Hanson deal that. Dad made me go out with his son, Richard, a couple of times and he kind of creeped me out. I didn't like him. He was really cagey about his family and how they knew ours... and I knew the boys hated him. Theo told me he was a... well a bad person, so I... I thought it would help, or at least buy me more time. I wasn't thinking straight. I wiped the diary with my jacket; under the desk too. Then I got out of there, but I still had the gun and... Oh god, you have to tell Charlene I'm sorry. Promise me, Dylan. Tell her I'm so sorry."

"Why hide it in her jewellery box?" Cooper asked.

"I knew it locked. And Charlene kept the key in the nightstand. I got cleaned up, cleaned the gun and got out of there. I was going to go back later and get it, but I thought *what if someone's found them already?* What if Dylan or George found them and the police are already there? So, I called Charlene and arranged to spend the day with her. I thought it would give us both an alibi. I tried to make it right. I didn't mean to frame her. I tried to tell you she wouldn't do that."

Lily was becoming increasingly anxious, and her doctor looked like he was ready to throw Cooper and Tennessee out of there.

"Try to relax," she told her.

Dylan stood, moved to the bed and sat on the edge so Lily could nuzzle into him. "The long sleeves and heavy make-up. You've been hiding the bruises he gave you, haven't you?"

Lily's head bobbed in and out of his chest. He protectively stroked her black hair and addressed Cooper. "It was self-defence."

"I know that," Cooper said. "But she'll still be charged." She felt for the young woman, and though she hoped the CPS would be lenient, forgiving even, she knew Lily's life would never be the same. She was going to have to live with this forever. "I'm sorry, Lily. Dylan, you should call your lawyer. He'll know what to do."

He shook his head. "I'll get someone new. Dad's lawyer was a tax and finance specialist. I wouldn't trust him with this. Not with you, Lily. I'll get you the best."

Cooper looked at Tennessee. He returned her stare with a bob of his head; it was time to let the young woman get some sleep and recover from her surgery.

Before leaving, Cooper thanked Dylan for his help while they'd been in the bunker. She couldn't know how it would have played out without him, but she knew he'd acted swiftly when they'd needed to carry Lily out of there. Thanks to him, Lily hadn't bled out. Tennessee held the curtain for Cooper. As she left, she reached into a pocket, retrieved a small white card and placed it on the corner of the bed.

When Dylan Blackburn was sure his sister had fallen back to sleep, he picked up the piece of card that the detective with the short hair had left, and walked to the window for some fresh air. He felt heavy with the weight of a crumbling family on his shoulders, but it was a weight he was determined to bear. He would save his siblings and breathe new life into the Blackburn name.

He took in the view of a fan-shaped car park and waited until the two detectives reached their car and drove away. Glancing down at the piece of card in his hand, Dylan turned it over. It was a business card: *Oliver Timms, Defence Lawyer.*

- Chapter 30 -

Gentle waves lapped at the shore. Bands of white were pushed up the golden sand by the enduring power of the North Sea. The sky was cloudless and bright, the sea, aquamarine with hints of grey. Longsands beach looked glorious. To the south, the ruins of Tynemouth Castle and the Priory loomed over the cliff face, and to the south, the steeple of St. George pierced the sky.

Cooper watched the water, almost hypnotised by the rhythm it held. In, out, in, out. A never-ending force. As sure as the Earth kept spinning, the tides would keep moving. Just like crime. One case in, one case out. As soon as one investigation came to a close, you could be damn sure another would emerge. With various Blackburns either dead or in custody, and with Hanson facing life for arson and manslaughter, Cooper hoped that organised crime in the region would take a dive. That was wishful thinking at best and pure naivety at worst. The Roker Boys or the Daytons would move in and battle over the remnants like scabby seagulls fight over chips. If she was lucky, there'd all take each other out and leave the city mob-free, however, she'd never been the lucky sort. Now that the Blackburn / Moradi case had drawn to a close, Cooper was feeling refreshed and physically lighter. She worried about Lily and what awaited her. She'd wanted to hunt a cold-blooded killer but had instead found a scared little girl who feared for her life.

A staging area had been set up at the south end of Longsands, next to Crusoe's café. Commissioner Begum from Northumbria Police and Chief Fire Officer Spence delivered speeches while spectators gathered for the charity triathlon. A representative from the Fishermen's Mission, a charity that provides welfare and support for fishermen as well as running services for lost seafarers, thanked Begum and Spence. He took the microphone, spoke about the important work of the Mission, and expressed his gratitude to those involved in today's fundraiser.

Cooper pulled her dressing gown tighter around her. Underneath it, she wore a plain black bathing suit that didn't entirely cover the impressive black and grey chest tattoo she'd recently acquired. The design of roses, complete with leaves and thorns, perfectly hid her lumpectomy scars and covered not only her breasts but some of her upper chest and shoulders.

The relay triathlon would soon begin. Cooper took her place on the starting line with all the other poor sods who'd been strong-armed into doing the swimming leg. All body types were represented, from hulking firemen to more heavy-set women who were giggling with each other to cover their nerves.

Elliot Whyte took the spot next to Cooper. "Good luck, ma'am." He removed his robe and added it to a growing pile. Cooper did the same. "Fuck me. It's colder than I thought. I'm freezing my fucking tits off." Suddenly his jaw fell. "Ah, shit. Sorry."

"Relax. It's just a phrase, and besides, I didn't have a mastectomy."

"Oh. Well, good." He looked away, fixing his gaze on the grey-blue that awaited them.

Cooper thought he looked uncomfortable so she couldn't resist making it worse. "And since when were you worried about hurting my feelings?"

Before Whyte could answer, a bell rung to signal the start of the race. Cooper didn't waste a second, she sprinted towards the sea, all the time wondering what the hell she was doing there. How had Tennessee convinced her to do this? Her feet met the shallows. *Jesus*. The water was icy cold. High-pitched squeals filled the air, and once the water reached groin level, the men felt their prized possessions rapidly start to shrink. Cooper tried to block out the cold, telling herself she'd been through worse, that cold water was nothing compared to chemo. The tactic worked and Cooper was soon deep enough to dive forward and begin swimming. She followed the route marked by buoys, concentrating on her breathing and maintaining a steady pace. The cold began to seep beyond her skin and chilled her to the bones. She'd kill Tennessee when she got her hands on him. He owed her big time. Sod it, he could look after Steven Seagull instead of Keaton.

Cooper had no idea how long she'd been in the water. Time seemed to slow down. Salty water got in her mouth and splashed up her nose, she spluttered and floundered but found her technique again. As she reentered the shallow water and her feet found the sand, she counted the people ahead of her. There were maybe six or seven, meaning she was in the first third. She couldn't see Whyte. Was she beating him? She hoped so.

Cooper ran up the beach, though waded or even plodded would be a better way to describe it. There was nothing glamorous about trying to run through shallow water or over soft sand, despite what the opening credits of Baywatch led you to believe. The sand clung to her cold, goose-pimpled skin, and each step she took was laboured. She was gasping for air. Tennessee was waiting at the end of the road that led to the beach. His arm outstretched, waiting for her to high-five him.

"You owe me a beer," Cooper said, panting as she slapped his palm with hers.

Tennessee jumped on his bike. "I'll buy you two," he said as he furiously began to pedal up the hill and onto the promenade.

"Make it three," she called after him.

Tennessee had to follow the road to the very top of Whitley Bay and back to the opposite end of Longsands where he'd find Keaton waiting for him.

Keaton would then sprint back along the beach to the finish line.

Now she'd stopped exercising, the chill really took hold, and her body began to shake. Despite her coldness, there was a great atmosphere on the beach. A steel band were playing, and a sandcastle competition was in full swing. Some of the sculptures were amazing. A huge coiled snake made of sand was so intricate the artist must have begun work in the wee hours, a fairytale castle decorated in shells stood taller than most of the children gathered around it, and a great sand sailing boat was beginning to take shape. Lifeguards were performing CPR demonstrations and encouraging members of the public to have a try on the dummies. All in all, the organisers had done a great job, and it was for an excellent cause.

Whyte appeared at her side, gasping and holding two dressing gowns.

"Thanks." Cooper grabbed her fluffy robe, shook it free of sand and wrapped it around her body.

"Listen, about what you said earlier. I know what you were referring to and I guess I deserved it. I should have had your back, but I didn't. I was a..."

"A prize dickhead?"

"Em, yeah. You know I don't really think like that. It was the environment. The station was a bit of an old boy's club back then."

"Translation, the station was a hive a misogynistic twats, and because you wanted to fit in, you threw me under the bus. I was fair game."

He scratched his head. "I regret it... Oh, Martin's overtaking someone. Where's Tennessee?"

"He's near the front. You can't miss him; he's wearing bright pink." But almost as soon as Cooper said it, Tennessee disappeared from view. He'd be back in around fifteen to twenty minutes.

"Mum!" Tina and Josh were running down the beach and had to dodge a boy of eight or nine who was having a massive tantrum. "I'm all packed! Can't wait to see Granny and Grandad. We'll need to weigh my bag though, it's full of textbooks. I might need to leave a few behind."

"Take as many as you like," Cooper reassured her. "We'll find space in my suitcase if need be."

Tina smiled. "Cool, thanks. I blended some fish to make enough feed for Steven for the next two weeks and got it portioned up and in the freezer. And I booked our taxi to the airport, and checked our travel insurance was still valid, and got some Euros, and... Oh yeah, we brought you some hot chocolate." She brandished a stainless steel flask.

Cooper hugged her daughter. "You angel. Hi Josh, how're things?"

Josh gave a nervous, mumbly answer that Cooper didn't understand a word of. Her hands were too cold to open the flask, so she asked Tina to pour her a cup. She gripped the lid as Tina filled it up with piping hot liquid. It smelled mouthwateringly good. It obviously wasn't the one calorie per cup crap.

"You were brilliant, Mum. We watched from the old pool."

The boy having the tantrum was now running away from his mother and trying to kick over every sandcastle that he passed.

It wasn't long before the first cyclists came back into view. The leading pack was about five strong and Tennessee's bright pink t-shirt was amongst them. Cooper bounced with excitement and began cheering for him, not that there was any chance of him hearing her. Tennessee leapt from his bike and ran down the bank that led onto the north end of Longsands. A group of runners jostled on the starting line, waiting for high-fives from their teammates. Cooper couldn't tell which blurred dot in the distance was Keaton, but she knew she wouldn't hesitate in barging a burly fireman out of the way if it meant giving herself a competitive edge.

The running leg of the race was just under a kilometre in length, but the soft sand would make the journey much more tiring than had it taken place on tarmac or grass.

"There's Paula," Tina said, pointing up the beach. "She's gaining on the man in third."

Keaton's legs pumped hard, causing plumes of sand to billow behind her as she ran.

"Come on, Paula!" Cooper cupped her hands around her mouth and yelled as loud as she could. "Yes, she's caught him. She's in third."

"The man in second is slowing," Tina said. "That, or Paula's getting faster."

A beefy man in too-tight shorts crossed the finish line to rapturous applause from the gathered spectators.

"They're neck and neck... Oh, come on, Paula. SPRINT... YES!" Keaton overtook the man in second and powered over the line. She didn't even look that out of breath. Cooper, Tina, Josh and Whyte ran over to her and showered her in congratulations.

One by one, more runners crossed the line, running into the arms of their teammates. Tennessee didn't take long to jog along the beach and reunite himself with what he had dubbed the Dream Team. His wife, Hayley, pounced and showered him in kisses. The action made Cooper smile; she hadn't seen Hayley so happy in a long time. A few feet away, Hayley's mother cradled little Alfie and chatted to Keaton's partner and brother.

"Well done," Hayley gushed at them all. "And Erica, I can't believe you went in the sea!"

Cooper was halfway through insisting that Tennessee and Keaton take all the credit when Tina handed her her mobile. "Mum, it's Granny."

Cooper took the phone and walked away from the group, covering her other ear with her free hand. "Hi, Mum."

"Hello, Erica. I'm just at the hospital." Julie's voice was distant.

"How's Dad? Flights are booked and bags are packed. Tina and I are due to arrive just before two tomorrow afternoon." She looked at Tina who was bouncing up and down, telling Keaton how to feed a juvenile seagull while the bratty boy destroyed the sand sailboat? *Where was his mother?* Her daughter had been through a lot. Some time in the sun would do her good, even if it wasn't under the best of circumstances.

"Oh. That's..."

"Do you want me to bring any goodies over? Yorkshire Tea? Marks and Spencer's chocolate?'

"Erica dear..."

Cooper could sense it before Julie had even said it. "I'm sorry, darling. There were complications with his surgery. The doctor said something about a clot breaking loose and causing another heart attack. He— He didn't make it."

Tears flooded Cooper's eyes. "What?" she asked. It didn't make sense. It just didn't.

"He died, darling. He passed about twenty minutes ago."

Cooper span to face the sea, not wanting the others to see the shock and pain on her face. Though she'd only seen her father a handful of times since he moved away, she always loved him, always missed him. The father-daughter bond had suddenly been snapped in two and the hole it left in her gut ached. Cooper felt as if she was falling.

"Oh, Mum." Her voice quivered then broke. She hadn't made it. She'd been too late and would now never get to say goodbye or tell him one last time that she loved him. What was wrong with her? She should have booked an earlier flight. She could have flown from Manchester or Leeds. She should have handed the case over to another DCI and been on the first flight out of the country the second Julie mentioned chest pains. She'd regret her decision until the day she died.

Sobbing into the phone, apologising over and over for not being there, Cooper felt more out of breath than she had done during her swim. She couldn't breathe. Behind her, an announcement was booming over a loudspeaker. *No. Not now.*

"And in second place, from Northumbria CID, congratulations to DCI Cooper, DS Paula Keaton and DS Jack Daniel."

"Boss?" Keaton saw the look on Cooper's face and tapped Tina on the arm. Tina instantly read her mother's mind and ran to her.

"She can't go up there," Tina urged.

Tennessee grabbed Keaton. "I'll go up. You stay here."

Tennessee took to the stage and collected an enormous silver cup and shook hands with Commissioner Begum and Chief Fire Officer Spence. He thanked his team, thanked Superintendent Nixon and tried to say something witty. Regrettably, no one was listening or watching Tennessee. Cooper's pained wails had attracted the attention of the crowd; her despair was too raw to stifle. Tennessee jumped from the stage to make way for the winning team from Tyne and Wear Fire and Rescue, but as his feet hit the sand, a scream filled the air. A scream loud enough to drown out Cooper's cries. Then another. And another.

All eyes turned to the undisciplined boy. He was staggering backwards, away from the sand sculpture of the snake. His eyes were wide; his mouth a perfect oval. He'd kicked a great hole in the side of the snake, and something protruded from the crumbling mound of sand. It was pale and bloated, and it was unmistakably a human arm.

DCI Cooper will return in Northern Roulette.

- MESSAGE FROM THE AUTHOR -

I HOPE YOU ENJOYED your time with Cooper, Tennessee and the gang. If you could take a moment to head over to Amazon and leave a review, it would mean a great deal to me.

All those moons ago, when I started writing The Only Weapon, I never envisaged I'd follow it up with a detective trilogy. Four novels down, and I'm still as excited about writing as ever. Would that still be the case without lovely reviews and messages of support from readers? Possibly not, so I'd like to start by thanking each of my readers for joining Cooper on her adventures.

Fans of northern noir may have recognised the reference to a crime family called the Daytons. The Daytons take centre stage in Shaun Baines's books Woodcutter, Pallbearer and Yardbreaker. This was my way of tipping my hat to Shaun for his support since I released The Only Weapon.

The Fishermen's Mission is a nationwide charity supporting active and retired fishermen. The fishing industry is at the heart of life in North Shields, and I'm sure the same can be said for numerous other coastal towns.

Roll The Dice would not have been possible without my mum, Liz, and my good friend, Amanda. They are always there to read the messy first drafts. Thank you both. The biggest thank you must go to my partner and best friend, Rob, for his continued support. His good humour has buoyed me during the more emotional moments of the Covid-19 lockdown, and his encouragement is a constant source of motivation. He has listened to ideas, not looked too suspiciously at me while I research how to poison someone, and when I've needed a shoulder to cry on, he has been there with his exceptionally good shoulders. I love you.

- About the Author -

Betsy was born and raised in Newcastle upon Tyne, living first in Gosforth, then Jesmond. In 2013, she moved to North Shields and enjoys spending time walking her Welsh terrier along nearby beaches and learning about local history.

At school, Betsy struggled with spelling and grammar. However, she doesn't believe in giving up on something because it's difficult. She finds writing novels can be compared to martial arts. They are both thrilling, exhausting, and rewarding.

It's no secret Betsy considers herself part ninja. She also works as a taekwon-do coach and is a self-confessed UFC geek. Her ideal Saturday begins with an intense workout, followed by a long bath, a spot of writing, steak and red wine, and then retiring to the sofa to watch the latest title fight. She came up with the idea for her debut novel, The Only Weapon In The Room, the morning after Rousey Vs Holm.

Betsy's writing process involves drinking ridiculous quantities of tea and hot chocolate, bouncing ideas off her friends and family and getting distracted by Twitter and TikTok.

- Be Sociable -

Facebook: B Baskerville - Author

Twitter: B__Baskerville

TikTok: B_Baskerville

Instagram: B_Baskerville_Author

Newsletter: You can subscribe to the B Baskerville newsletter using the form on BetsyBaskerville.co m. You'll mainly hear from B when she has something to share, such as a pre-order going live, a new book release or sale etc.

- Also By B Baskerville -

The DCI Cooper Series:
Cut The Deck
Rock, Paper, Scissors
Roll The Dice
Northern Roulette
Hide & Seek
Finders Keepers

Stand Alones:
The Only Weapon In The Room
Dead In The Water

Printed in Great Britain
by Amazon

38149518R00162